I'LL
GO
ON

TRANSLATED BY

I'LL GO ON

HWANG JUNGEUN

EMILY YAE WON

TILTED AXIS PRESS

소나기 Sonagi

A sudden, brief downpour; a cloudburst. The three
syllables of so-na-gi ('gi' is pronounced with a
hard 'g') are echoed in the names of the three
characters, Sora, Nana, and Naghi; and the word
itself is an abbreviation of the initial title given
to this novel – *Soranananaghi* – when it was first
serialised in *The Quarterly Changbi* between
Autumn 2012 and Summer 2013. 'Soranananaghi'
has an incantatory quality to it, as though uttering
it will bind and protect the trio – as an umbrella,
frail and embracing all at once, provides a shared
if imperfect refuge from the weather. A quietly
defiant symbol of solidarity.

SORA

小 蘿

My name is Sora.

The ra in Sora means water parsley, and in Hanja is written 蘿. They'd meant to use the character for fruit, 菰, but my grandfather bungled the listing on the family register, and fruit became a herb. Though I'm told he enjoyed the flavour of minari, so it could simply have been a matter of taste. I mean, ra 蘿 and ra 菰 look nothing alike, do they. So you couldn't honestly claim to have mixed them up, could you, Grandfather. In truth, I barely remember my grandfather. When I was two years old he caught a fish in the river, ate it, and died of hepatitis; there was hardly time to become acquainted. From what I can gather he was a man of average build, average strength, and average means, and everything he did was deemed pedestrian.

—

Listen.

Your grandfather didn't die from eating the fish, my mother would say.

There was a flood, see.

In the flood, a lot of homes were lost and quite a few people lost their lives, too. But your grandfather, he had to go fishing in the middle of all that chaos. Entire homes and beasts and men and women are being swept away, and he's stood there casting his line in the muddy roiling water. What killed him was the water he dredged that fish out of. Think of those lives caught in the raging current, the grief they must have felt, the anguish. And he's angling away in that same water. That's the sort of man he was, and that's what got him killed. It was the bile of the folk whose cheeks and backs were scarred by that hook of his that choked the life out of him.

—

Mother's name is Aeja.

And Aeja is how Nana and I refer to her, instead of as Mother. It suits her better to be called by name: the ae in Aeja means love, and true to the name she'd been full of love, practically brimming with it.

Aeja's capacity for love seems to have reached its peak during her courtship with Father. Nana and I've heard her recount those days time and time again. Many of the stories were of summer, this being the season they'd first stepped out together.

We were hit by a massive typhoon, one of those rare storms that occur once in a hundred years, she would tell us.

The winds blew so hard they tore through shop signs, toppled telegraph poles, uprooted entire trees.

The two of us, though, we walked clean through it, our clothes barely ruffled. On we went – a single umbrella between us – stepping over splintered boughs and entire roadside trees that had split down the middle, some right in front of our eyes. Twigs lashed the air like bones and arrows, but nothing touched us, we were unharmed, we walked on.

But what did you do on those walks? I asked her once.

There was a long pause while Aeja turned the question in her mind, then she replied, we talked.

What they'd talked about she could barely remember now, only that they had, and endlessly.

How could you have said so much and not remember any of it, we would demand, to which she would simply say, because.

Because I held and clung to his words so dearly and fiercely they seeped right in, straight inside my body, leaving nothing to memory.

Inside your body?

I wasn't listening so much as devouring, see. I drank and ate his words until there was nothing left to remember, because by then they'd all become me, a part of my body.

You know how that sip of milk you have in the morning fattens up your blood and muscles? Well, that's how his words and his stories got to be in my blood and in my bones, Aeja said, after which she seemed to sink back into her thoughts.

—

There's a photograph of Aeja from that period of courtship.

In it, Aeja is young and pretty and smiling.

It's taken at a fairground and there's an orange streak across her face from strolling under brightly coloured canopies. She stands with her back to a merry-go-round that's a swirl of melt-in-your-mouth candy shades, her chin lifted towards the photographer in a dazzling smile. Her bobbed hair is sweetly dishevelled, soft curled locks kissing her neck, her skin pale, her brows dark, her lips red: she is the spitting image of Snow White. And next to the beloved Snow White stands Father, who either shifted the moment the shutter clicked or was caught on camera mid-motion, for half of him has already walked out of the right-hand corner of the frame while the rest of him grins at you from a blurred, partly turned face. This is the only photograph Nana and I have of Father. Aeja did away with them all. Did she devour them too, I sometimes wonder. Did they all end up as blood and muscle and bone like those stories of his?

In the photograph, Father is showing his teeth, so he must have been laughing out loud. I wonder about his laughter, the timbre of his voice, the accompaniment to the words that wound up in Aeja's veins and bones. We did live together for the first ten years of my life so the whisper of it should still be there. I recall the toys and the sandals I'd had then; surely his voice must be in there too, among the jumble of memories.

This is what he would've sounded like.

This is what he would've sounded like, I'll tell myself as I conjure up a specific tone, but the confidence to assert, yes, that's my father's voice, just isn't there. I must have heard him call out my name hundreds of times in the ten years we'd lived under one roof, yet I'm unable now to summon it. Watered down over the years in a steady barrage of sounds, it's simply – gone. Sora-ya, he would have called out to me, or so I tell myself as I try to bring his voice back to my mind's ear, but it's no use.

Sora-ya.

Letters are all I see, black strokes surfacing before me as on a sheet of paper.

—

Father's name was Geumju.

His family name was Kim, so he had double the gold, in kim 金 and geum 金, in his name.

That's something of a girl's name, isn't it, may have been a comment that followed him around in childhood, since the other half of his given name, ju 紬, means silk.

Nana was nine and I was ten years old when Father died. He was sucked in beneath a huge cogwheel in the factory where he worked. The upper half of him had been crushed beyond recognition by the time he re-emerged, and it's said they had to take a roll-call of every employee left on the factory floor before they could figure out who had had the accident.

Aeja was the one who told us this story.

Listen, she'd say.

We'll be happy, the four of us, that's what he used to say as he slaved away day and night.

Your poor father.

What was the point in trying so hard.

Numerous times Aeja repeated this story to us, and after each retelling she'd add, that's life for you, in an instant it can all come to a screeching halt, and that's that. Your father died a tragic death, yes, but not because he was exceptional in any way.

It's just the nature of life, she'd say.

Futile to the end – that's human life for you and there's no use fighting it.

—

This year, I am the age Aeja was in the photograph.

Aeja is still pretty, if no longer young. Which isn't to say she's old: it's more a matter of dwindling rather than ageing. I don't mean to suggest her arms are spindly or her body's shrivelling up, only that the immaterial part of her which must be lodged some- where inside is drying up, depleting from one day to the next to a wizened kernel. All it'd take is a nudge, a gentle jog of her shoulder as she sits in some sunny spot, and out it would clatter like the husk of a walnut from between her ribs.

Trifles and things of no consequence.

If you mean to go on, you'd best fill up the world with such things, Aeja says. This was the gist of the many stories she fed us from our earliest childhood. Aeja's stories are soft as spun sugar. In honeyed, subtle tones, she speaks of the resentment that fills the world and how living in it brings nothing but sorrow; of how we all bring suffering upon ourselves. Truth be told, there's not a scrap of meaning to be found in this mortal, mortal, mortal world. Not an earthly thing worth the fuss. All struggling gets you is more grief and heartache. All that to-do, only to have life halt in some senseless tragedy, or to meet a slow, miserable, meaningless end, snared in an illusory murk of supposed joy and significance. When death is death, however you come at it. Dead and done, and that's all there is to it.

Dead and done, nothing more, Aeja says.

In the same breath, she'll speak of the lingering bitterness that fills the world.

But if dead and done is all there is, if death is so final, then why should anything remain. Why should rancour, itself, remain? There's an inherent contradiction to what she says that becomes apparent as you listen, but as long as you're in the grip of her words you can't help but be taken in. I shouldn't be paying any heed, you tell yourself, even as the words latch onto you. You're not even aware of being swallowed up in the machinery of her tale, it's only later that you'll realise with a jolt – hang on a minute – I've been lured in again. That's how it generally is with Aeja's stories. They're as potent as a putrid peach or the most enthralling of poisonous spells. Listening to her words your head starts to droop with their sticky juice trickling down your ears, until all you can do is succumb to the saccharine flow. The most bewitching of her concoctions are the ones that tell you that to live is to suffer and therefore you need not suffer especially when things take a bad turn; that it's okay to be numb to the pain; that there's no use trying, since life is by definition futile. Hence the numbing trifles and things of no consequence.

And in a world made up of inconsequential trifles, what is there to cherish, why hold anything dear?

Or so I've been thinking lately.

Sora is my given name.

The ra in Sora means minari.

The idea was to use fruit ra, except my grandfather bungled the registration and I came to be named after the herb instead, or so goes the tale as Aeja has told it to me. And this being a tale told by Aeja, it may not be true at all is what I've been thinking lately.

Forget the fruit; maybe I was meant to be a minari

all along.

—

I came across a beautiful danpung leaf, its colour so radiant I couldn't bear to look straight at it.

This was in a dream.

I felt a breeze and heard the maple rustle its red leaves, and then I woke up.

Perhaps the dream had not been intended for me, perhaps it was one of those dreams you have on someone else's behalf. This thought didn't dawn until the following day. And although an entire day had passed in the meantime, the image of that leaf remained so vividly etched in my mind that I couldn't not mention it to Nana. When I did, she remarked that perhaps it had been a taemong, a dream foretelling pregnancy. I hadn't had sex in over a year so I didn't stop to consider whether such a dream might apply to me. Instead a fleeting thought crossed my mind and I looked over at Nana, wondering if it could have been intended for her. Nana sipped her barley tea with an inscrutable expression before asking, wouldn't a danpung leaf mean it's a girl?

Why's that?

Well, the bright colour for one.

Then it must mean a boy, since it's the male birds

that tend to sport brighter feathers.

The conversation veered off course and I didn't get a chance to ask if the dream had been about her. Instead we headed out for work, and stood side by side at our usual stop, until in no time at all our buses arrived to bear us along our separate routes. As I sat and reflected over the morning's exchange it seemed to only grow in significance, but since I couldn't very well get off the bus and chase after Nana, I continued on, before eventually stepping down at my customary stop. This was in a neighbourhood where another fifty metres along the road stood a boulder marking the provincial limits. I paused for a moment under the signpost announcing its single bus number before starting up the wide and gentle incline.

The entire area had been put up years ago to house displaced people in need of relocation. Many of the homes shared the same orientation of front entrance or slant of roof as though they'd been assembled all at once, quite possibly by a single construction outfit. And though it was an old neighbourhood, the houses with their attics and yards made up a trim row along the streets, which in turn were tidy and well-maintained with no signs of shabby, crumbling corners. I'd been surprised to note that the usual crop of redevelopment sites – a sure sign that spring had arrived – was absent here, until my boss, the president of Good Construction, informed me of the regulations restricting such work. Continuing on along the streets, I wondered if the necessity for thrift and upkeep was what had kept the neighbourhood in as decent a shape as this. In any case, it was a tidy grid. And if one were to take an aerial view of it, would it be an oppressive sight or a beautiful one? An oppressive one, I supposed. These thoughts flitted through my head as I ambled up the hill. The ground was slick from a recent dose of water, but whoever was responsible for it seemed to have retreated indoors. Not a soul was about. The neighbourhood was, as usual, serene.

Winding my way up the slope, I recalled how the first time I'd passed these streets on my way to the job interview, I'd been incredulous that a construction firm specialising in tipper truck rentals would have its office in such a tranquil and isolated residential area. Good Construction was located at the dead-end of a street. Burrowed into the low-lying hill, the office had most likely served as a home garage or storage space before being repurposed. The entrance was overhung with trailing ivy, giving the overall impression of a dugout or shelter that I, for one, didn't mind in the least.

This morning it appeared I wasn't the first to arrive. The door with the pasted-on letters spelling out *Good Construction* was ajar. I guessed isanim, our director, had come in early, and so he had. He was at his desk reading a newspaper. At Good Construction, each member of the firm was tasked with a single responsibility according to their title: president, director, manager, or keeper of books. The office itself was windowless, and one door served as the sole air vent and opening in the poky room. Within this cramped space four desks had been arranged to each face east, west, south, and south, respectively; to one side were a low coffee table and a sofa, and at the back was a narrow and dimly lit space that served as the office pantry. The president and the manager were frequently out of the office, entertaining clients or conducting meetings and site visits, and with walk-ins being few and far between, it generally fell to the director and me to man the office for entire stretches of the day.

The director's name was Isa.

I am not making this up. The director's first name – Isa – just happened to be identical to his title – isa.

Odd, isn't it.

The strangest of coincidences, I know, but that really was his name. He went by Mok Isa and also by Mok isa. Having neither a degree in architecture nor any on-site experience, he was usually strapped for things to do around the office. He'd only been roped in by our president, who happened to be his brother-in-law, for two reasons: his name, and his ability to bankroll the place. The rest of the time it fell to him to read the paper, follow the sports broadcasts, wipe the orchid leaves, and stand and gaze out the door to while away the day. Maybe it really was a pregnancy dream: I found myself unable to let go of the niggling thought even after the workday had begun and, mulling it over at my desk, I did an idiotic thing. I unwittingly wrote out the words *Nana is pregnant* on a piece of paper, only the director happened to see it.

The day had been unremarkable. In the sweltering sun the glass pane at my back had become intolerably hot by noon. Every time the door opened and shut, a pulsing block of torrid heat heaved its way in. Outside, the creepers cut deep, dark shadows. The phones rang intermittently with routine queries for the contact information of this or that building site, and lunch was invariably delivered to our desks. Outwardly everything was as it usually was, whereas inwardly I'd been in turmoil all day.

Nana might be pregnant.

I mused, staring at the dim cement wall of the pantry. Nana might be pregnant, I repeated from behind my desk, looking blankly at the phone extension of the fax machine as I wondered what to think about this potential scenario.

Nana is pregnant, I wrote, not realising what I was doing.

Then I thought to myself, but that's not even a question. Surely the first step is to determine *whether* she is; surely, I'd meant to write *Is Nana pregnant?*, or was I already fleshing out the plot as if it were a given? When there was no way I could even remotely be sure that she was carrying a child. Engrossed in these thoughts, I was frowning at the words, pen gripped in hand, when:

Who's Nana?, I heard a voice ask and looked up to find the director standing next to me.

Before I knew it, I'd crumpled up the note, shoved it in a drawer, and slammed the drawer shut. It was rude of me, perhaps, but for that matter, so was poking your nose in other people's business. If anyone's overstepped the line here, it's him, I thought to myself, feeling my cheeks flame. The director stood silently for a moment before returning to his desk.

Who is Nana?

My little sister, of course.

My little sister Nana. Who may be having a baby.

Is it okay to say that of a baby? That a mother *has* a baby? Are babies something to be had, to have? Is the baby the mother's to have? Should a baby be someone's to have? To have a baby: to say that of a child feels somehow not right. It feels very not right. It's unsettling. Stifling, even. Is it better to say she's carrying a child, or that she's with child? Or, simply, that she's pregnant? Pregnant: Nana may be pregnant.

I suppose the best thing is to ask her if she is.

———

I'd resolved to be upfront about it the next time I saw her, but in the days that followed I found myself unable to broach the subject. I would meet Nana at home after work and circle around her until, having failed to ask the question, I'd head off to bed. This continued for some days. I noticed that Nana was avoiding both alcohol and coffee. Instead she seemed to have developed a fixation with persimmon leaf and camomile infusions – who knew where she'd even got her hands on such things. On the whole, she appeared to be watching what she ate and drank. Was it because she was, in fact, pregnant? Was she taking precautions because she was now with child?

At other moments I would see her being very lax: for instance, eating an entire Japanese Spanish mackerel followed by another half-portion in one sitting, while I looked on with mounting anxiety. Because, little sister, I think I heard somewhere that one should steer clear of blue-backed fish in the early stages of pregnancy.

And that it's especially advisable to do so these days.

But far from making such meddling comments I was unable to even formulate the original question I had intended to ask, and instead continued to simmer in silence with each passing day.

Exhaustion set in from having to face Nana as she sedately went about her business, blithely unaware, or perhaps aware yet uncaring, of my dilemma. I realised I was starting to resent her possibly feigned obliviousness to the weight of my own burden. So on that Friday night, I chose to drop in at Naghi's store instead of heading home after work.

Naghi had a tiny bar on a corner of a decidedly quiet street. A hole-in-the-wall, the space had originally been a single-car garage that had been converted into a shop selling chipao and Chinese-language coursebooks before Naghi took over the lease. Naghi inherited the failing spot, fixed it up, hung up a sign that read *Wage*, and started his business. Wage served beer and a limited number of anju dishes. It was Naghi who made the food, served the food, and cleared up afterwards, and the number of dishes on the menu was determined by the workload he was able to handle. Up to five people could sit at the counter, facing the kitchen with its ladles and its strainers for fishing out noodles, and the bar would be at full capacity. The shape and size of the place meant you had to brush past the backs and behinds of people seated next to you if you were to use the restroom, for instance, and this was the one complaint I had when visiting Wage, that even in its dimensions the place so closely approximated the English word *bar* – a stick, basically – admittedly with the added space of kitchen and worktop and a modicum of seating space, but even so, more a slit of a corridor than an actual room.

Naghi adhered to two simple principles in running his business. The first was to only use fresh ingredients, so that not letting the day's supplies go to waste became a necessary extension of the rule. The second was to never serve food that he himself would not eat. Simple, I say, though in fact this seemed to me a pretty costly way to run a business. But Naghi was resolute.

On days when patrons were few and far between, he would cook up what remained of the day's ingredients and drop by Nana's and my place. That's no way to run a business unless you mean to run it into the ground, Nana would say, but her tone was never harsh and Naghi for his part didn't seem to mind Nana's gentle chiding.

Nana might be pregnant.

At my words, Naghi raised his head in surprise.

I saw a danpung leaf in my dream, I added, and went on to describe the conversation I'd had with Nana days earlier. Naghi listened, then nodded his head and agreed that it may well have been a pregnancy dream. But then he asked me how I knew the dream was about Nana.

Well, because, I said. I have a gut feeling.

A gut feeling?

Yeah, like a hunch or an intuition, I said.

At this Naghi slid the tip of his knife into the raw fish laid out on his cutting board to deftly shave off a sliver of its pale flesh before remarking, it could just as well be about you though. Me? No, nope, there's no way... not me... not when I haven't had sex for the past year, I nearly said in response. In all honesty, I hadn't so much as held or been held by anyone in all that time, let alone had sex. Truth is, I have a strong aversion to being in too close a proximity to anyone; I loathe physical contact of any sort. The only exceptions to the rule are Nana and Naghi — I don't mind being physically near to them, or occasionally touching or hugging them, as Nana and Naghi are well aware. So to tell Naghi, of all people, that I hadn't had sex in a year... well, it was quite unnecessary.

Wrapped up in my own thoughts, I was sitting with my head bowed when Naghi placed a white plate in front of me. A glistening rolled omelette sat in its centre. Being rather small and plump, it resembled a miniature yolk-coloured floor cushion, and was flawless: perfectly evenly done in silkiest yellow and neatly portioned into bite-sized pieces. I picked up a piece with my chopsticks and put it in my mouth. Delicious. But then Naghi's cooking is consistently delicious, so much so that it's easy enough to concede the pride he takes in knowing that he's an excellent chef. Even a simple rolled omelette proved the point. What set his dishes apart were the particular essences he coaxed out of the plainest ingredients. The food he cooked up had that elusive quality that could only be described as the presence of flavour. The presence of it, yes, that's exactly it, I thought as I sat savouring the omelette. Meanwhile Naghi had started on the dishes. Listening to him wash up, I continued to steadily work my way through the rest of the omelette.

You unhappy about it?, Naghi suddenly asked from across the worktop.

No, I'm good.

You're good?

Yeah, this is really tasty.

Not that, I was talking about Nana.

Nana?

Are you unhappy that Nana might be pregnant?

I frowned mid-bite. Unhappy?

… I'm not sure.

I haven't really thought about it in those terms, happy or unhappy, so I don't know, I answered. But as soon as I'd uttered those words, another question jostled its way to the front: had I not been able to ask her because when it came down to it the thought galled me? I fell knee-deep into this new question, as though stumbling into another pit when I had yet to grope my way out of the first one. Unhappy?

Am I unhappy about it.

Is that why I can't ask her about it.

Maybe I can't seem to ask her about it because I find the very notion of it disagreeable.

Is that the case?

Maybe I *am* unhappy about it.

I'm not wild about the idea of a baby.

I'm really not.

In truth, I hate it.

Yes – yes, it's true. I hate it, if I'm being honest.

Because it terrifies me.

Because if it's actually the case, then I'd have to start worrying – about everything.

Isn't Nana worried?

About everything.

What was she thinking, getting pregnant?

I'm starting to feel short of breath now.

I'm furious, in fact.

What was she thinking, I ask myself.

Except it's not out of concern, as in, what will she do. No, it's out of indignation, as in, was she even thinking.

Has Nana set her heart on becoming a replica of Aeja.

Is that it, Nana.

You want to be another Aeja?

Fall in love like she did, and make a baby, and then have the baby, all so you can turn into an overbearing mother?

Like Aeja.

It was all I could think about on my way home. That I couldn't stomach the idea. It sickened me to even think it, I finally admitted to myself. Then resentment took over. Night had fallen and it was dark now, but the stifling heat wouldn't let up. In the muggy air, even the moon looked soiled. That's right, soiled, I thought spitefully. I staggered along the gloomy, heat-radiating street, my face a ghost, my mind consumed by loathing.

Nana was at home. She sat at the table, staring vacantly at a cup of steeping persimmon leaves. Hair still wet from the shower, clinging to her youthful face and back. The damp strands of it leaving darkened patches on the mauve shirt that served as her pyjama top. Scruffy girl, I tut-tutted to myself.

To think she might be having a baby.

What was she thinking, I repeated to myself.

But on this night, too, I was finally unable to ask the question, let alone speak to her, before miserably trudging off to bed.

—

Listen, Aeja said.

It must have been a very big cog, mustn't it?

A big thing meshed to another big thing that was pinioned and snarled into gears both smaller and larger than its circumference? And even the smallest of them, they must have been really, really hard? No matter the size, each wheel would have been made of steel and therefore impossibly sharp? And all of this to form one great constellation of endlessly orbiting machinery? Immense but intricate, the first cog aligned to a larger cog that set in turn a whole body of other bigger and smaller gears in motion? Whirr, whirr, whirr? So that one rotation led to five rotations and five rotations led to twenty-five which led to six hundred and twenty-five turns of the wheels... and the six hundred and twenty-five rotations would set three hundred ninety thousand, six hundred and twenty-five rotations in motion... and the three hundred ninety thousand, six hundred and twenty-five turns would feed one hundred fifty-two billion, five hundred eighty-seven million, eight hundred ninety thousand, six hundred and twenty-five rotations... which in turn would propel two gigantic revolutions... which would engage numerous smaller pinions...? And in each and every one of these rotations, no matter how numerous, each tooth of each wheel must have gnashed together so very precisely and powerfully? As scrupulously and as brutishly aligned as the clenched jaw of a beast? After all, that's how they're supposed to operate, that's how we've designed them? To grind away in perfect calibration, without the slightest gap that could jeopardise any of its spinning parts? Whirr, whirr, whirr, whirr, the machine must've purred, each day like clockwork, unerring, absolute, snug in its impeccable timing, mustn't it?

Listen.

Inside and around that circuit of rotating, inter-
locking parts – that's where your father ended up. At
first, it was probably something very small. Something
as random as a loose thread on a sleeve. Something
that caught at the gear teeth. A mere trifle, that's what
snagged him. But everything that followed after...
well, each of those things would have been bigger,
harder, narrower, and more intricate than the last. Did
he have time to cry out? Or was there no time even to
say *oh*? Who's to know? Maybe time passes differently
in the middle of all that meticulous grinding. Maybe
it stretches out and what is supposed to be an instant
lasts for so long that you couldn't possibly fill it with a
single *oh*. Maybe even a drawn-out *ohhhhhhhh* wasn't
sufficiently long enough. Maybe that's how long the
instant lasted – for much, much longer than any of us
would've ever imagined possible. And when eventually he had passed through all the toothed parts, well,
the sound, it would've no longer counted as sound.
The shape of him would've no longer counted as a
shape. To have tried so hard only to end up as that.
That's human life for you, to end in naught. Listen,
when a person doesn't amount to the smallest blob
but is shattered and scattered and formless, is all but
a mere smattering, a scant handful of dust – where,

then, is the person? What, then, is the person? When all distinction of this and that part is gone and the neck I touched, the shoulders I clung to, the elbows I held, the eyes I looked into, the rounded chin I'd stroked, and the warm head, and the voice – that voice, the voice that called me by my name and called you by your names, and the body behind that voice, thinking remembering sensing – yes, my love, the body of my love – when that body finally emerged in what couldn't possibly be bodily form, where then in that moment was, is, he?

Where is the soul?

———

I've been having recurring dreams about the house I grew up in.

In the dream, I'm tracing endless circles inside the empty house.

Circle round this corner of the wall and I find myself in the house next door.

Circle round the other corner and I'm back at our house.

I'm all alone in the dream, turning loops for what seems an eternity.

But there's someone there – on the other side of the wall.

I feel a presence and hurriedly whip round the corner, but whoever it is has already vanished around the other end. I follow in pursuit and make another darting turn, but the stranger eludes me. I twist and twist around the wall for some time, in vain. At some point I realise the other person's no longer there: I'm spinning circles round the empty house on my own. In the dream, everything feels far away and there's a murkiness overhead so that I can't tell where the ceiling begins. It's chilly and dank on either side of the wall, and each time I turn a corner a strand of my own hair winds about my neck and I gasp with surprise.

And all the while I'm thinking, but we lived in a house exactly like this one.

Before, Nana and I had lived in a house just like it.

The year I'd turned eleven.

The year after our father Geumju ssi passed away, by which time Aeja and Nana and I were poor and had to move out of our home. Our father's family pocketed the entire death settlement under the pretext that since my mother hadn't borne sons there was no one in our family to take care of jesa, the rites held in honour of the deceased. Besides, they claimed that they'd been against our parents' marriage in the first place. This, and Aeja's general apathy to practical matters, meant the three of us had nothing left to fall back on. Soon the lease for the house we'd shared with Father was up and it was time for us to vacate the premises – and still Aeja showed no signs of preparing for the move, instead spending entire days in a cocoon of her own thoughts. Only when the actual day arrived did she finally call a rag-and-bone man to come and have a look round the place, and then, on condition of handing over all of the remaining items in the house, managed to borrow a small pushcart from him. Aeja packed two bags and two boxes into the cart and walked out of the house without a single glance backwards. Nana and I shouldered our overstuffed school bags which we'd crammed full of textbooks, pens, pencils, exercise books and the like, and trailed alongside the cart. After a half-hour on foot we arrived in a quiet, unfamiliar neighbourhood. Lined neatly along the street were two-storey houses with old-fashioned exterior staircases and balconies. Aeja continued on past several of these houses only to stop in front of one that seemed more or less identical to the one beside it, and parked the cart. We pushed open the blue metal gate and stepped into a clean dry yard laid with reddish bricks, across which was a sash door leading to the semi-basement. This was the entrance to our new home. Aeja opened the door with a tiny key, and Nana and I peered inside and were met by a curious sight: the semi-basement was split length-wise down the middle by a wall.

This space had likely served as a storage cellar before each floor of the house was converted into separate units and the basement floor itself subdivided – by erecting the centre wall – and leased out to two families willing to share the entrance and bathroom. Perhaps that doesn't give you the clearest picture. What I mean to say is, the flat had a wall that had intentionally been left unfinished. It effectively split the space in two, but the wall didn't extend all the way to the back where the common bathroom was. Instead, it stopped just short of the hall. Or, to put it another way, the tenants on this and that side of the wall were not residing in self-contained individual units, but occupying one half of a single partitioned unit. I've mentioned that the front door and the bathroom were located at either end of the wall. This meant these two features belonged partly to the right-side and partly to the left-side half of the flat. Bizarre, I know, but such living spaces do exist in this world.

Aeja took off her shoes in the hall, shuffled further in towards the left, and neatly lay her body down in the empty room. Pale legs gathered together, hands clasped against her chest, eyes gleaming, nails long and limpid as fish scales. Nana and I put down our packs and waited by Aeja's side, combing our hands through the locks of her hair as they spilled out on the floor. Aeja's eyes stared blankly up at the ceiling for what seemed a very long time. Then out of nowhere she called to me.

Sora-ya, she said, do you remember the way we came?

I nodded.

The cart, can you return it?

Return it where?

Back to the house.

Could you go return it, she asked, and so Nana and I set off together.

Nana insisted on climbing on back so we took turns pulling the cart while the other rode behind, Nana struggling when it was her turn to pull, and by degrees we arrived at the old house – only to find the front door ajar. Aeja had always been vigilant about locking up, and Nana and I, who had never, not even on the hottest summer days, seen our front door flung wide open, were spooked by this unexpected sight. We hung back, not knowing what to do. Nana begged me to let us leave the cart where it was and head back, but I held on to her and peeked inside the door.

The old ragman was kneeling on the kitchen floor, rummaging through the cabinets. He hadn't bothered to take off his trainers and the baggy knickerbockers around his legs were caked with muck and dirt. Next to where he knelt was a grimy grease-soaked basket holding Aeja's bottles of condiments. I could read the labels written out in Aeja's hand: *soy sauce, vinegar, salt*. The floors Aeja had kept meticulously clean and wiped were now streaked with the ragman's filthy footprints. Everything that Nana and I had touched and used while living here lay in a heap in one corner of the living-room floor, and there was a pile of clothes on the threshold of one of the rooms. The pile resembled a tumulus or, rather, a mound of shed bodies, as though people whittled down to mere skin had fallen one atop another in successive layers. The sight chilled me to the bone.

I turned then and fled, walking towards the new house as quickly as my feet would allow. Quickly, quickly.

I took care not to break into a run, though. I felt I shouldn't, somehow; I had a premonition of sorts. Something was about to happen, I thought. That something was what lay ahead of me now, along this road stretching out before me. It may have already happened or perhaps it was on the verge of happening, but the moment I broke into a run it would inexorably come to pass. I could feel it. And once it's done it won't be able to be undone, I said to myself, not even aware what *it* was. Quickly, quickly. I strained forward. Quickly now – hurry. Nana with her shorter strides kept falling behind, but still I hastened forward, I couldn't wait, hurry, quickly, quickly. When we finally reached the house, we found Aeja exactly as we'd left her, staring fixedly up at the ceiling from her spot on the floor. Legs buckling, I slumped to my knees by her side, and immediately wet my pants. The gentle flood of urine along my thighs. Warm and soothing. I considered it a stroke of luck these weren't tears I was leaking. Tears were difficult to conceal, whereas the wetness in my pants might go unnoticed, unaccompanied as it was by overt sounds or signs that had to be stifled or held back. I would not be found out by Aeja. With immense relief, I settled down on the floor.

—

It was a large space.

There was room to spare.

There was no wardrobe, no desk, no bed, no table, no fridge. Only the three of us, Aeja and Nana and me, in a semi-basement that felt as subterranean as the ceiling was lofty, the air cool to the skin and smelling of moss or mushroom. Eventually Nana and I picked ourselves up from where we'd been lying on our bellies waiting on Aeja, and played a game of open-and-unpack-boxes. There was no coherent method to our laying out items on the floor, and once all the boxes had been unpacked there was nothing more for us to do. We found Nana's drawing paper and my colouring pencils and began to draw. I would draw a tilting tree and Nana would add on a branch. I'd sketch in a green mango among the foliage (What's that? A mango. What's a mango? It's a fruit. When did you see one? A long, long time ago. Did you try it, Unni? Of course I did. What was it like? Sour, and pungent. Pungent? Mangoes are pungent. Then why would you eat them? People eat them when they're unwell. It's a fruit for sick people.) and Nana would perch a red bird on a branch. I'd outline a long, slender stem to which Nana would attach a yellow flower in full bloom, then Nana would conjure up a horse and I'd stick horns onto its head. We drew pages and pages of this stuff. And by the time we tired of it and ventured beyond the front room to explore the rest of the house, evening was setting in. Nana and I stood in the hall with our backs to the front entrance and peered down the long, narrow space. The gathering dusk dappled the length of the tall middle wall.

Nana and I passed the kitchen and opened a door into a sizeable room. This was to be ours, probably. We walked once around the room; we opened the dusty window. Looking out the window, our eyes met the ground: cemented, with dried pools of water. Less than a metre away stood the neighbouring house, its wall blocking the view so there was no glimpse of sky – or anything else. Instead, we saw a moth. It had attached itself to the wall opposite. It had a fat belly and ashen wings that were big enough to maybe cover Nana's entire eye. Apart from fluttering its wingtips in the occasional breeze, the moth showed no signs of movement. For days afterwards it remained glued to its spot, until one day we found it had simply vanished, leaving behind a light-brown lint-like stuff which Nana and I believed to be its egg case. Every so often we would open the window and observe it for any signs of tearing or rupture caused by baby moth larvae emerging from it. The lint was all clumped together, a tiny island unto itself, and it hung on, even in the rain. Nana and I began to think that moths typically required several days to lay eggs and that those eggs took years to hatch. What tenacious creatures, we marvelled.

Forget tenacity – that moth was just long dead is

all.

Looking back, isn't that the most likely scenario?

A sickly moth landed on a random wall to deposit its eggs, then died before it could. Out of sheer exhaustion. Still it remained on that wall, if only as a shell, an increasingly hollowed-out shell, until one day, a wind bore it off. That must be what had happened.

That's all it was, probably.

Only barely managing to leave behind an egg case.

An empty case at that, since the moth never did get around to filling it with eggs or whatnot.

For Nana that moth may be a distant memory by now, if she hasn't entirely forgotten it. I think about it though, from time to time. Its triangular body, small against the light-blue surface of the wall. It had seemed large at the time, but must really have been quite small. Naturally.

Are you dead or are you alive?

In certain moments, this is what I ask the moth.

Dead or alive.

When in answer to my own question I think it is long dead, the memory of the clarity and vividness of its wings, despite their ash-grey colour, resurfaces to cast doubt; and when I answer it's living yet, the memory of the moth's enduring stillness makes me

sceptical. Does such a moth exist? One that lays its
eggs over several days and whose eggs, once laid, can
take years to hatch? Though I must admit I've never
since come across a moth resembling that particular one, so perhaps it was an atypical moth after all.
Assuming such a moth does exist. One of that specific
physiology. If it was no average moth we saw, then
let's call it a moth unlike any other – but does it in
fact exist?

Which are you: dead or living?

–

Nana and I met Naghi in that house – in that same
house where we discovered the moth, on that same
day. We'd crossed over to the other side of wall. We
hadn't planned it or even realised that was what we
were doing, and yet there we were on the other side
of it. Easy-peasy. All it took was a few steps. Walk a
few steps, turn the corner, and there you were.

Around the corner it was a little bit warmer and a
little bit darker. I recall having smelled something dry
and brackish. Kelp, maybe. And there was the quiet
hum of a refrigerator. This side of the wall had the
same layout as our side: a room, a kitchen, another
room. The dividing wall was the axis from which the
two symmetrical spaces spread out like a butterfly's

wings. The only difference was that here, unlike over there, we could feel the full presence of sounds and warmth and all the necessary paraphernalia of daily life. It didn't occur to me or to Nana that we were trespassing; we gawked at the space like two spectators as we shuffled along the wall, until we found ourselves turning the corner back to our side. It was uncanny. A left side and a right side, with a wall in-between. When we stood with our backs to the front door, our place lay to our left; but standing at the other end with the bathroom behind us, we'd find our place had shifted to the right.

Left, then right.

Right, then left.

Nana and I continued to circle round the wall, our right hands trailing along its surface, passing from here to there and back again. As though winding thread around a gigantic spool, round and round we went, until, on our umpteenth round, we saw a boy standing in the living room of the other unit. He wore an old T-shirt that had a picture of a sailboat on it, and from under his neatly trimmed hair which covered his brows a freckled nose jutted out. This was our first encounter with Naghi.

Dokkebi.

That's what I thought you were, Naghi would

later tell us.

He'd been napping, so he'd tell us, when he became aware of the patter of footsteps, a persistent loop of bare feet pacing to and fro between the long-empty space next door and his own home – what else then, if not a dokkebi, some trickster bogey out for mischief?

That was how the story would come to take shape some time later, but the actual conversation on the day went like this:

Dokkebi, the boy blurted out, at which I turned as pale as a sheet.

Did he say dokkebi? Nana whispered, clinging to my side. Unni, this house has dokkebi?

The boy gazed silently at Nana before nodding and said, of course. Though I haven't seen one yet.

How do you know, if you haven't seen one?

I just do.

How?

Because this house... it has strong yin energy, the boy said earnestly.

Nana and I looked around us, bewildered. The pooled darkness of the ceiling and the heft of the wall we'd been encircling seemed to take on menacing dimensions.

I spoke up: What does that mean, to have strong

yin energy?

    It means you have dirty thoughts.

    Dirty thoughts?

    Dirty thoughts, all the time.

    And dokkebis like those sorts of places?

    They're dokkebis, after all.

    What are you, then?

    What are *you*?

    I'm Sora.

    And her?

    Nana.

    I'm Naghi, the boy said.

    How'd you two get in here?

    How did we?

    Well, we had a key, didn't we.

    A tiny key.

—

After this oddly disjointed conversation which ended our first meeting, Nana and I returned to our portion of the house and thereafter took care not to cross over to the other side of the wall on a whim. But the shared features of the house meant morning and afternoon encounters were inevitable, whether it was right after you'd been for your first pee or as you crouched over the laces of your tattered trainers. Whatever the circumstance I couldn't help feeling a bit flustered; but as these chance meetings grew in number, the three of us gradually got to be on speaking terms, if only to exchange a few perfunctory words. Sometimes one of us would lose our key, and when that happened we'd plop down on our schoolbags outside the locked door and do our homework while waiting for the other key to arrive. Naghi was small then, and young, though he's not small any more, nor young. Nana and I were small then, too, but not now, we're not kids any more.

The key was small.

It had a reddish hue and a short piece of frazzled yarn knotted around its head. It felt small even in my ten-year-old hands and I suppose it still would in my grown-up hands. As an adult, I've tried a few times to describe the space that key allowed entry into, but generally these attempts have not gone well. Even when I'd somehow succeed in explaining, the usual response would be one of scepticism. People would demand to know how such a preposterous house could realistically exist. Was it so preposterous? Since I found no pleasure in pursuing this line of thought, in time I simply stopped speaking of the house. But in any case, and perhaps thanks to its layout, the rent on that house remained unaffected by the general rise in rental value in the neighbouring properties for a number of years, allowing us to stay put for a relatively long stretch of time.

At home and outside of the home, Nana and I were unfailingly at each other's side. On our way to and from school, of course, but also on lunch breaks; at times we even sought each other out between classes. Any chance we got, Nana would come and meet me or I would go in search of her. And once reunited, we waited: for school to be over, or for someone to turn up and tell us, their face creased with worry, to hurry on home. Always being together meant we were always set apart as a pair, a solitary team of two, but we were too preoccupied by the thought of Aeja to even notice this.

Aeja was all we thought about.

In the new house Aeja was, on the whole, kind and gentle, but she was also on pins and needles.

She showed no great interest in what Nana and I ate, whether or not we brushed our teeth twice a day, what clothes we wore to school, or whether we had clothes fit for the weather. Sometimes she could bustle about for an entire day or two, cooking up mountains of grilled toast with ham and egg or surprise eggbreads until we simply couldn't stomach any more of it; for the most part she was despondent and spent hours at a time in a deep torpor, lying flat on her back, her face arranged into a doll-like expression. Then there were the rare occasions when she would leave the house by herself and not return for days. Nana and I tried to stay as close to hand as we could, wishing to remain by her side, our beautiful and kindly Aeja who was nonetheless gripped by an emptiness that fuelled her apathy. We did our best not to bother her or be a burden to her, foraging on our own for food and clothing like a pair of docile little beasts.

That winter, Aeja left home one day and did not return for an entire week. We woke up around midday to find her gone, with only a few banknotes left under a half-full litre pack of milk in the middle of her room. This was nothing new. Nana and I stood in silence in Aeja's vacated room for a moment, but soon we were washing our faces, tidying up the house, and sitting down to eat. With the money Aeja had left us we decided, after some discussion, to buy mandarins. There was a fruit truck parked a few streets away, selling mandarins at one or two thousand won a bag. We bought four bags, two per person. There were roughly thirty small mandarins to a bag, but the shiny orange skin was so pretty to look at and so much fun to peel off that we managed to work our way through all four bags in just two days. On the third day, we found some stale rice cake lying about since who knew when and decided to reheat it in the rice cooker. We tipped the whole thing into the pot and waited; when we finally opened the lid the steam was dense and the hardened white mass of glutinous rice had spread out on the bottom of the pot like the softest, stickiest glob of porridge. The smell that wafted was off, but in colour and in texture the rice cake looked appetising. Nana and I spooned up the piping hot injolmi, dipped it in sugar and each took a bite. The sharp taste that filled our mouths made us hesitate, but we found that once we continued chewing, the taste became more tolerable.

Just then Naghi's mother appeared from across the wall, exclaiming, my goodness, what is this I smell, it sure smells sour.

What is that you're eating?

Naghi's mother strode into the kitchen and peeked inside the pot. Back then, Nana and I were still calling her Gran, Gran from next door. Unlike Aeja, Naghi's mother had a dark complexion and broad shoulders. Her eyes were wrinkled and her hair was bunched up in tight little curls like all the other grannies.

Let me have a bite then, she said, and tore off a piece of the hot rice cake with her bare hands and popped it into her mouth.

I could feel my cheeks flaming. I was ashamed to have been caught eating spoiled food, mortified that I'd been feeding it to my younger sister, saying in an offhand tone, it's all right, isn't it. I was also oddly embarrassed that there were no grown-ups at home. Looking back now, I still couldn't tell you for which of these three reasons I felt most humiliated that day. Behind my clamped lips the rice cake lay hot and sticky on my tongue, but there was nothing I could do about it just then. Filled with dismay, all I could do was watch in dread, certain she would spit out the rancid injolmi at any moment.

Naghi's mother glanced round the stark kitchen, chewing all the while on the rice cake, and then turned towards Nana and me, as we stood there with sugar on our lips, and looked us over carefully. To my surprise, she swallowed the rice cake, and told us that this injolmi was so delicious she'd like to exchange it for some of their food. With that she led us across the wall to their home.

From that day on, Nana and I began to eat meals cooked by Naghi's mother – not at every mealtime, but quite regularly nonetheless. In those days even primary school pupils had to bring packed lunches to school. Naghi's mother would prepare two additional dosiraks and set them on the shoe cabinets, one on theirs and two on ours. Nana and I picked them up each morning on our way to school. At lunchtime we would meet by the corner bench out in the yard with our dosiraks and sit down to eat together. As lunch boxes go, these were rudimentary: next to the rice we would sometimes find an entire grilled croaker with its head still stuck on, or a heaped serving of spicy pickled cucumber; occasionally a rolled omelette would accompany this instead of the usual fried egg; at times there were no sides at all except for a fried egg sitting atop some rice sprinkled with seasoned soy sauce. Nonetheless, Nana and I prized every meal. Considering how young we were at the time, I'd say those lunch boxes were what fed our growing bones. If bones had growth rings, that period of growth fuelled by Naghi's mother's food would have left indelible marks on ours, Nana's and mine both.

In a sense, then, Naghi and Nana and I are inextricably linked by having shared a common source of sustenance, like potatoes that draw nourishment from a single root. If Nana and I have an almost nostalgic reaction to fried eggs and lightly charred grilled fish, it probably stems from our memory of this particular period in our lives – all the more so considering that

Aeja was never one to grill fish at home, even before Geumju ssi's death. My hankering for a plate of perfectly grilled fish and the rush of emotion I get each time the taste of it passes my lips are therefore entirely due to those precious lunch boxes, and due to Naghi and his mother.

Packing three lunches in the morning.

As a working woman at that.

I came to understand what an impressive feat that was only after I'd become an adult myself.

My first job straight out of high school was at an office located in a run-down commercial building in the city centre, and finding an adequate lunch spot nearby was a trial. You'd think otherwise, it being the city centre and all, but oddly there were barely any restaurants around. Our office was on the fourth floor, and when lunchtime came around I would order a typical baekban set of one main dish and an assortment of sides served alongside rice and soup at the fifth-floor cafeteria. But the doenjang soup with its scant handful of chopped onions and cubed tofu was too salty and the rice was of such a bleached-white colour it was verging on blue. The stainless-steel food tray, spoon, and rice bowl uniformly gave off a stench of a powerful washing-up liquid (bleach, I suspected), and regardless of what was on the menu that day, all that was served up seemed to reek of it. Everything on the tray, including the food, was coated in the harsh odour of it, so that the entire meal smelled of detergent. It got to a point where I had to surmise that the reason all the dishes in this particular restaurant were either overly salty or overly spicy was due to an attempt at camouflage, to conceal that very smell and taste. Here was food devoid of all flavour, soul, and life. Enduring a daily diet of such fare for the sole reason that there were no alternatives to be found was sapping away all my appetite, including my appetite for life. I won't put up with this any longer, I finally told myself, and from that day on I began packing my own lunches.

At first, I couldn't have been more ambitious. I'd make rice with an assortment of grains and beans I'd left to soak overnight, prepare three different braised and stir-fried side dishes and even pack clear broths which were simpler to whip up. But gradually I eased up to a more basic mix of barley and regular white rice, and it didn't take long before I was passing on the barley, too. Then the side dishes underwent a similar fate, pared down to the basics of kimchi, egg, raw tofu, and toasted laver, and as for soup, I increasingly had to forgo it for lack of time. It dawned on me that ten minutes of a morning was an altogether different affair from ten minutes of an afternoon. Time not only had a distinct flow in the morning, it was tinged with a particular meaning at day's beginning.

More importantly, my dosiraks didn't tally somehow. They defeated expectation, and chillingly so. Imagine anticipating a hot lunch, a temperature of eighty degrees, only to take the first bite and realise that the actual degree of heat was closer to fifteen. Imagine how bereft you'd feel in that moment. Well, this was how I felt eating the meals I'd gone to such trouble to prepare. I just haven't got the knack, I told myself. But that wasn't all. My glaringly limited repertoire — the number of side dishes I could concoct — dealt another blow to my will. Right, then. If food doused in suspiciously chemical smells and my own home-cooked lunches both resulted in the same dispiriting loss of appetite, then I may as well as slip in a few minutes of extra sleep in the mornings. So I packed it in on the packed lunches. All in all, the labour had lasted two months. In the six months that followed before I quit my job altogether, I fell back into the depressingly routine diet of flavourless, soulless, and lifeless fare. Though the identity of my opponent remained unclear, I had admitted total defeat.

—

Naghi's mother is called Sunja.

Sun as in the character 旬, for some reason, which means ten days.

But what was it about Sunja ssi's lunch boxes — what had been their secret?

It was only after my short-lived lunch scheme met a dead-end that I finally thought to ask myself this question.

Sunja ssi made a living selling fruit at the market, and her earnings had built a life for her and Naghi. It was gruelling work: she would leave home at the crack of dawn, be rushed off her feet all day, and return long after dusk had fallen. How weary she must have been. Their lives weren't free of financial hassles either, since Sunja ssi's husband, who had suffered a stroke while lifting a crate of apples one midwinter day, had left behind a substantial debt. And yet every morning, without fail, two lunch boxes were set out for us on the shoe cabinet, flat and square. This continued until the day Nana and I moved onto a school that did provide free meals — some six years later.

How we relished those packed lunches.

However simple and unadorned they may have been.

What's the secret, I asked her once.

Sunja ssi looked over at me before replying, experience.

Meaning age?, I asked her, but she told me it was not as simple as that.

It's all in the hands. Feeding and raising your own leaves a mark. Like rings on a tree.

Right, then, I thought to myself.

Can't feign something like that.

Even if it's something as ordinary as a lunch box.

An ordinary lunch box we could unfailingly rely on.

To have tasted this first-hand, to have been fortunate enough to experience this kind of dependable consistency – even to this day I ponder the significance of this, the fact of it and what it means. What if we'd never had that presence in our lives. This is a hypothesis I'm reluctant and even fearful to flesh out. Because I don't doubt that it was Sunja ssi's dosiraks that nurtured us and fed our very bones. Without them, our bones wouldn't have amounted to much; they'd have been paltry, feeble things at best, both structurally and emotionally impoverished. It's quite something, isn't it? To have raised what was bound to be meagre and sapless into something not quite so unsubstantial after all.

Above all, they allowed us a glimpse of something other than Aeja's world, something that gestured beyond what we knew.

That was their secret.

They were the plainest of lunch boxes.

Plain and commonplace. And yet to have contained so much in such a compact form is nothing short of immense. This is what I believe.

—

Hands that have fed one's own.

Will I ever come to have such hands?

For Nana it's a possibility. She may already be laying the groundwork for it. Back when we were eating the food Sunja ssi had made for us, Nana and I were small. We're not small any more. That's how much time has passed. Buoyed on those currents, I grew up, as did Nana. And now Nana's all grown-up and may soon be a mother. Perhaps she already is. Hands that have fed one's own – there'll come a time when she gets to have those hands. Sooner or later, the day will come.

But it won't for me. It won't, since I refuse to become that person. That's what I tell myself.

To be a mother is to be like Aeja.

To have a child is to be a mother, and to be a mother is to become Aeja. That's how my circuit's been set, twisted or not. Not so much in the way I think, but in the way I feel.

And so it's best not to make a baby in the first place.

As long as there's no baby there's no mother-to-be, and as long as there's no mother there's no Aeja. Not anymore. It's better that way. Aeja's to be pitied, yes. She's pitiful to such a degree that she's almost loveable, but it's better if she's not around – better if she's not in the world.

I am, and will remain, Sora.

I mean to end my days as Sora.

To become extinct.

The last of the tribe called Sora.

—

It hasn't rained in quite a while.

That was my first thought when I saw the open umbrella on our veranda that morning. It was a green umbrella that resembled a forsythia, but a closer look revealed the pattern of plump seal-like creatures. Nana was probably the last one to use it before leaving it out there to dry, seeing as it belonged to her. It was long dry by now. I held it up, intending to fold it away, and felt instantly erased.

The umbrella spread its ribs over my head.

Beneath the waterproof canopy, the ribs supporting its taut tension were visible as were the joints fixed in place by several tiny screws. One or two of the screws were eaten away. Around the most severely corroded of these was a ring of diffused rusty water. And so this too will rot and decay, I thought, until it disintegrates. As I stood inside the umbrella, gazing impassively at the tiny screws, all sound dissolved as did my sense of reality. Everything seemed to fall away: I was reduced to a pair of eyes. I could make out what I was looking at, but everything else was still. The umbrella was merely an umbrella, it bore no relation to me, and was silent.

Were I to vanish, mightn't the umbrella also disappear?

Probably not.

Geumju ssi had observed any number of things, too, while he was alive, but those things had remained intact rather than being erased away with him in death. Things don't just vanish: this is mostly, if not entirely, true. Neither Aeja nor Nana nor I had vanished.

Only he had.

As I stood there mulling under the umbrella, its insides grew steadily darker and wider until it seemed to take me over. There I was, on the cusp of not being there at all, feeling pinned down under the umbrella. Until only the umbrella remained.

There was only the umbrella.

That and nothing else.

What if umbrellas were all there was, would that be a blessing?

No Aeja, nor Nana, nor me, but a world composed solely of umbrellas.

If all suffering and pain were to disappear, leaving only umbrellas in their wake.

What would that be like?

Would it be good?

Good or not, what would it matter, when umbrellas are all that remain? When I'm no longer here to determine either way, then the question would be moot. A world where umbrellas are all that's left can't possibly matter to me. If it doesn't matter, why care about it. And yet, I wonder, what would it be like? A world where nothing matters, what would that be like? Would it, somehow, be good? Would it be good if the world were that way - should the world be that way?

—

Days passed by and I remained unable to ask Nana my question.

It was the height of summer. The torrid radiating heat fired up the days and nights, and midday temperatures soared to well over thirty-six degrees; with every stifling breath I took it felt like I was gulping down hot air. Yet, somehow, I'd managed to catch a cold in the midst of this dog-day heat, and was sniffling constantly. I couldn't seem to shake it off. I'd be shivering one moment, swept up in waves of fever the next, then further disorientated by an icy chill creeping up my limbs to the pit of my stomach. The medication barely seemed to have an effect, and I spent a succession of days in a dazed stupor at the office, feeling not so much ill as depleted.

Sora ssi.

I turned around at the sound of my name and saw that the director was sitting on the guest sofa. He was slouched over a dressed-up cardboard box. Having opened the box, he carefully extracted a cake of considerable size and carefully placed it on the table. A bit of birthday celebration, I thought..., he mumbled in my direction. It's not my birthday, I answered automatically, at which the director looked at me with a puzzled expression before letting out a chuckle.

Not yours, Sora ssi, but mine. It's my birthday today.

The cake was summer-themed. A girl with an inflatable pool tube stuck under her chest floated in a sea of whipped cream dotted by several large, fresh-looking strawberries. The director opened the slim, vertical envelope that came with the box and fished out a few candles from it which he plunged into the cake. Two long ones and five short ones: five and twenty years? As if sensing my scepticism, the director said, I told them I didn't care how many candles they gave me and this is what I got. He grinned sheepishly. I watched as he drew the match and lit the candles. The office was ablaze in the full afternoon glare and the flames appeared small and insignificant. If it's his birthday, as he says, should I be singing the birthday song now, I wondered to myself. I was still hesitating when the director himself broke into song. *Happy birthday... happy birthday...* I followed along in a small voice although I ended up mumbling the last line as it made my toes curl to address him, even in song, as dear anything. When the song was over he remained still, gazing at the flames as if deep in thought, and then, starting from the farthest candle, blew them out with three short successive breaths.

As we lacked appropriate plates and forks, we improvised with chipped tea saucers and disposable wooden chopsticks. The director gulped down his slice of cake and tucked into a second. I'd never seen him eat anything with such gusto, and I wondered what had got into him today as I finished my own plate. Blobs of cream were smeared on the saucer, alongside the strawberry that had topped my slice of cake. I debated whether or not to eat the strawberry then used my chopsticks to halve the fruit before putting it in my mouth. It seemed the director was eating his too: I could hear the faint crunch of seeds. I was quietly listening to this sound when the director stopped moving his jaw and asked me:

It's not to your liking?

I'm sorry?

Is there something off with the taste?

He started smacking his lips together as though trying to taste what he'd been eating all along.

Is it the strawberries, maybe?

No, it tastes like any other strawberry... But why do you ask?

You were frowning.

Oh, I was just thinking.

About what?

The fact that you eat strawberries.

...Yes, I do. Is that strange?

No.

What then?

Nothing, only...

Yes?

It's just... I know someone who doesn't eat strawberries, and I guess this reminded me of that person.

Yeah?

Why don't they?

Sorry?

Why don't they eat strawberries?

… You're quite insistent.

You'd rather not say?

Yes.

Well if you'd rather not say, then why bring it up in the first place? You can't make a person curious about something then not tell them, that's unfair.

No, it isn't.

You won't explain this aversion to strawberries.

I wasn't talking about myself.

Precisely.

Well, this person who doesn't eat strawberries… it's someone who happens to be the son of a fruit seller. And every night, his mother would bring all the leftover fruit back home with her. The fruit she couldn't sell any more. So they'd always have a stock of fruit at home, but whether apples or plums or whatever else, these would without exception be bruised or squashed and could only be eaten with the skin removed. Having been raised on this, he came to believe that was how fruit was meant to be eaten. So now, even when the fruit's fresh enough to be eaten whole, he feels compelled to remove the skin. Apples, peaches, plums: the lot. His physical and emotional memory insist that the skin of these fruits is inedible, and when he does attempt to eat a whole fruit, he says strange things happen to his body. And strawberries are of course the most ambiguous for him, since the boundary of skin and flesh is so unclear, and this baffles him.

Really?

Yes.

So that's a thing.

It is.

And who is it?

I'm sorry?

The person who doesn't eat strawberries, the one who used to be the son of fruit sellers.

That, of course, would be Naghi, I thought to myself.

It was Naghi I'd been thinking of.

The tiny key, and the boy with whom we'd shared it.

And from whom I first learned of the tribe called Sora.

———

Take Nana, for instance — Nana hates soy sauce.

This, I think, was how that particular tale began.

At twenty-five, Naghi left to live in Japan for a spell, having got wind of a potential job there. The day before his departure Nana and Naghi and I all gathered at Sunja ssi's to cook and share a meal together. We started with the rice and side dishes and soup, moved on to fruit, paused for some tea, and once we felt able to, had some more of the remaining fruit. But then Sunja ssi belatedly remembered the dough she'd prepared the day before – and soon we were cooking up the chewiest, most toothsome sujebi dumplings, and somehow devoured the entire pot of sujebi with repeated exclamations of *delicious*, *delicious*, scraping the bottom clean, before once again finishing off with tea and fruit – all this over the course of six hours, a non-stop marathon of eating and drinking that culminated in Sunja ssi going to bed and Nana falling asleep right there at the low folding table, her legs stretched out along the floor, leaving only Naghi and me awake.

As I recall, it was around this time of year, a summer night.

It was now well past midnight, and through the door we'd left flung open the night fog seeped in. The beer turned lukewarm in no time and the faint aroma of cooled cooking oil hung over the living room.

Nana snored occasionally. A moth hovered ahead, rubbing its wings on the fluorescent light. Naghi was scratching his arm with one hand and peering down at the table. I was pretty drunk by then, I sat and waited for his next words to follow.

Take Nana, for instance – Nana hates soy sauce.

Having said this, Naghi drew the tip of his finger on the sweating beer glass and touched the table, leaving a drop of moisture on its surface.

This is Nana.

I forced my drooping eyelids open and peered at the tiny drop of water.

That's Nana?

Nana. Nana who hates soy sauce, Naghi answered earnestly before making another dot beside the first one.

This is Sora.

Me?

Sora who likes soy sauce.

Finally he made a third dot with the remaining moisture on his finger and claimed it for himself. This third one was smaller in dimension and not as tidy around the edges, having been made after the first two drops.

And that's you?

That's me. Since I neither like nor dislike it. For

me, soy sauce is a black liquid – nothing to like or
dislike. That's how I see it. See how even among the
three of us here our preferences are at such odds? We
don't even agree on something as simple as soy sauce.
Each of us answers differently, because we're different.
In both trivial and important ways. In other words,
I belong to the tribe that is indifferent to soy sauce
whereas you, Sora, belong to the tribe that likes it,
and Nana belongs to the tribe that hates it.

Tribe, I repeated to myself, looking from one
transparent dot of water to the other.

Na, Nana, Naghi. Me, Nana, Naghi.

But…, I opened my mouth to ask. How can it be
a tribe? Without any tribespeople to speak of?

There's you though.

Me?

You're both tribe chieftain and member.

Even when there's only one of me?

Single-member tribes do exist in this world, you
know.

—

Naghi has grown to like soy sauce now.

Or does he.

It might be more accurate to say he's become
adept at handling it.

Is handling something well the same as liking it? Could you say the two are one and the same?

Or is it not the same thing at all?

He can incorporate it into any dish with measured deftness and subtlety. He's developed a real flair for it, and I like this version of Naghi, the Naghi who knows his way around soy sauce. I like him just as much as I liked the Naghi who said soy sauce was merely this black substance to which he was indifferent. To like someone or something just as much as a previous iteration of their being is truly remarkable. There aren't that many things in the world about which you can claim to do so, regardless of the nature of the change they've undergone. I think it's remarkable, really. Naghi's remarkable. Just as Sunja ssi's packed lunches had been.

When I think back to how that evening wound down, there's not much that comes to mind. In a half-sleep I heard someone say, I'm off then, and opened my eyes to see Naghi packed and ready to go, standing in the living room. He was wearing a short-sleeved shirt and jeans, and next to him was a suitcase that was even smaller than I'd expected. Not bothering to wake Nana, who was sound asleep, Sunja ssi and I went and stood outside the front door of that house to see Naghi off, both of us looking pretty haggard.

See you then, Naghi said.

And with a wave of his hand he set out into the dark dawn, his suitcase trundling beside him. I heard Sunja ssi sniffling beside me in the dim light and wondered briefly if she might be crying, but she was calmly casting her tired but dry eyes in the direction Naghi had disappeared into.

Two years later Naghi showed up wearing the same clothes and lugging the same suitcase as on the day he left. His physical appearance, on the other hand, had altered to such an extent that he barely resembled the person we'd seen off that day. A mere two years had elapsed, yet it was as if he'd been gone for ten, flung into some dark strange corner where he'd been abandoned for all that time and had only now, just barely, made his escape to return home. There was a disc-shaped bald patch near the parting in his hair, and he was missing an upper canine tooth. But what had conspired to leave him in such a state he wouldn't say, a quiet smile sealing his lips no matter how much we asked him about it.

———

There's a grocer's called Good Super in our neighbourhood, the director said to me. And once I started to pay attention, I realised that there are actually a whole bunch of shops that have Good in their names.

Is that so.

Good Laundromat, Good Hair Salon, Good Pharmacy, Good Bakery.

As does our company, now that I think about it.

That's right, Good Construction.

Why do you think that is?

I'm not sure.

I really wonder. What do you think is the reason, Sora ssi?

The reason for...?

The reason there're so many businesses with Good in their name.

Well, I suppose because they want to make good.

Want to make good?

Maybe things aren't good for them now, and the name is meant to bring luck.

Good, make good... I suppose that could be a reason.

Yes.

There's something I've been meaning to ask. You always seem so preoccupied – can I ask what's on your mind?

Do I?

Yes.

Well, I suppose... I'm thinking about the good things.

The good things?

The good things, I repeated.

———

Listen, Aeja would say.

Good things are well and good.

People can't get enough of a good thing and when they find it, will fuss over it to no end.

The reason good things are given such a rarefied treatment is because that's what they are – rare.

They're praised and fussed over for being so scarce in this world.

There's not a whole lot of good, when it comes to it.

So you shouldn't live in hope of it.

The greater the hope, the greater the disappointment, and the pain.

Having said her piece, Aeja packed a handkerchief and comb into her bag that clasped shut by clicking together two metal beads, and left for the care home. The care home Nana and I were bringing her to, with its sunlit hill and its pond full of real lotuses. Whether Aeja was pleased with this arrangement or not, I couldn't say for sure. Better to say I'm not cer-

tain. Better to say that than to insist she was or wasn't
pleased about it, since Aeja herself hadn't voiced her
preference either way, hadn't said so much as a single
word, in fact. So: I'm not certain. Not to mention all
of this took place two months ago.

Let me think back to that evening.

Aeja was there, Nana was there, I was there. Nana
had just returned home from work and still had her
tights on under her skirt.

I can't go on having you here or looking after you,
Aeja, she said without batting an eyelid.

Instead she sat and faced Aeja squarely, her eyes
wide open and defiant. The blouse she had on was a
little tight and creased across her chest. Poor Nana. No
doubt Nana would weep if I ever said this, but she's
ruthless, I thought to myself. She's ruthless, and this
only makes her pitiable. Poor Aeja and poor Nana.

The following weekend we got Aeja into the backseat of Naghi's old car, and with Nana riding next to
Aeja and me in the driver's seat, we headed for the
care home, looking for all the world as if we were
out on an excursion. Aeja held her chunky knitted
bag of multi-coloured yarn on her lap, her face to the
wind. The rest of her things sat between my legs in a
large paper bag. Naghi found the hilly entrance to the
grounds without too much trouble. At the front door

of the care home stood a squat camellia tree, holding on to its few remaining, ragged flowers. The moment we entered the reception area, Aeja alighted in front of the padlocked ice cream freezer by the reception desk, leaving her bag perched on its lid while she peered at the contents.

It says two family members are required to give consent before Aeja can be admitted, so it's a good thing there are two of us, Nana said as she wrote down her name on the consent form. With a fierce grip that blanched her nails she wrote out her name in a crisp, neat hand, then handed me the form with the same wide, unblinking eyes she'd turned towards me a few evenings before.

Look, ice cream, I heard Aeja say.

While a nurse led Aeja here and there to measure her weight and blood pressure, Nana and Naghi and I trailed behind with Aeja's belongings. Deprived of sleep and of food, and having survived too many overdoses of her antidepressants when Nana and I had not given her our full attention, Aeja's body had become so gaunt it seemed a single blow would break her. In the reception area Aeja answered the head nurse's questions with indifference before following her inside. Nana and Naghi and I waited behind. Another nurse appeared soon after and asked to see

Aeja's belongings. Naghi nudged the paper bag out of my arms and opened it up for the nurse to see. The nurse removed anything that was sharp or breakable, or could be folded to form sharp edges or made into a loop or was tough, before ripping the cord handle itself from the bag, so that what she finally took away was a paper bag reduced to an envelope.

Nana and Naghi and I had to wait a while before being allowed to go up and see Aeja. The room she was given had an iron bed and there was a picture hanging on the wall that had been framed without the usual glass glazing. Through the window you could see the allotment plots of chillies and the bamboo forest beyond. Aeja was seated on the bed. She had tidied up her wiry grey hair into a neat bun. She pointed to the picture on the wall.

I've no use for such things, please take it away, she said.

Naghi climbed onto the bed to remove it. In the picture Christ was holding out his gashed palms to a throng of people gathered on a hill.

Goodbye.

This was all Aeja said in parting.

Nana and Naghi and I took the picture and left the room, then dawdled for a bit in the garden. Under the lotus leaves I could see the roots that extended down into the blackened oily lake. The sloping dirt path had dried clean and was marked with the traces of a broom. The soil in the chilli plot was reddish-brown; a black bee hovered over a red pansy. In the clear weather all this was glaringly, eye-wateringly visible. On the drive home I lowered the window, praying the wind would bear away any remaining traces of Aeja's words and presence. Nana and Naghi were silent. The air gushed in and rattled through the car, surging around us and making it difficult to breathe. Vanishing, I thought. I'm vanishing heart first into a colourless, scentless numbness.

That's all you'll ever get in this world, Aeja's words rose up and instantly bore me away.

Things of no consequence.

If you mean to go on in this world, it's best to think that's all there is to it.

—

What's on my mind every day?

The good things, of course.

The good things.

—

I'll ask her.

Tonight I'll finally ask Nana, or so I'd made up my

mind, but the question popped out, unbidden, on the way to work, as we headed to the bus stop.

The mornings hung heavy with fog, but for days the rains had failed to show. It wouldn't be long, though; I could tell rain was imminent. It was so exceedingly humid, merely standing still you'd be covered in a slick film of sweat. And the thing about fog is, there're all kinds of smells mingled in there. The fog, and the streets that were steeped in the fog each night, were shot through with the stench in the air, the myriad odours that grew stronger each day the rains didn't come. On this particular morning, too, there was a strong whiff of it on the way to work. It was early in the day and already muggy. Nana and I kept to the shade as much as we could, but that didn't stop the sweat from plastering the hair at the nape of our necks. In the oppressive heat the sweat felt cool against my skin. We followed the narrow street in silence, sometimes a step behind and sometimes a step ahead of the other. We were passing some cherry trees, their leaves spread thick and green, Nana just a little ahead of me, when I blurted out, are you pregnant? As soon as the words left my mouth, I was astonished by how easily they'd tumbled out. It was so simple, had taken a mere instant; all the days I'd spent hemming and hawing now seemed quite absurd.

I am, Nana nodded.

I'm on my way to the doctor's now if you feel like coming along?, she lobbed straight back, and, taken unaware, I found myself agreeing before I'd even had a chance to consider.

After a quick call to the office to say I wouldn't be coming in until the afternoon due to a personal emergency, I stood alongside Nana in trepidation and waited, and then it was time to follow her onto a bus I'd never once been on and then again time to scamper down the steps as she disembarked. Nana was in her usual work attire of beige blouse and black skirt that day. Looking for all the world as though she was on her way to the office and it was a morning like any other, she crossed the road with the assured gait of a person who's certain of her destination, headed straight for the maternity clinic, pushed opened the door, and strode into the lobby. The refreshingly cool air of a pleasantly climate-controlled space embraced us: by the time we'd crossed the lobby, my sweat had dried. Next to the lift there was a wide basin of flowers, an assortment of big carnations, roses, and peonies, all of them freshly cut. On the ivory walls framed paintings hung at appropriate intervals, subtly revealing their colours in the indirect lighting. Soft, cushy-looking sofas were dotted throughout the space. Everything, in short, had an air of ease, comfort, sophistication. I, on the other hand, felt ill at ease. I was disoriented and unnerved, discomfited and yet unable to admit it to myself. As I pictured it, giving birth was primarily agony and blood and screams, so to see this genteel, light-filled space, carefully put together to present an image that was as far removed from the truth as possible, was, I admit now, getting the better of me. I saw it as a blatant lie, a false claim to safety and snugness, an irresponsible way of suggesting you were in the right hands.

Regardless of my misgivings, Nana marched from one exam room to another, never faltering as she turned this then that corner for the various check-ups: blood, urine, ultrasound. She explained that today she had a few more tests than usual. In every exam room we entered there was an adjoining waiting area that at first sight resembled an art gallery, where pregnant women sat on broad sofas awaiting their turn. When we reached the ultrasound room, I sat Nana down and fetched her some water. Only then did I allow myself a cone-shaped paper cup of water. Young mothers-to-be flicked through magazines in the soft glow of the room. There was something that set this waiting room apart from the others, a difference I couldn't quite pinpoint and had to rack my brain to try and identify; but after some scatty, muddled attempts, I found I'd lost the thread entirely. Now all I could think was how I couldn't make head or tail of the situation, how I couldn't see what to do next. Can't grasp what to ask Nana. Can't tell what I can and cannot ask.

How do you feel now there's a baby in your belly, Nana?

That was the gist of my question, to which Nana answered, well, bloated.

Bloated?

It's like there's a giant sprout in my belly, she said, folding her empty paper cup in half.

A sprout? I turned the word over in my mind and looked at Nana's stomach. Two wide folds ran down the front of her skirt, and you couldn't really make out the bump. A woman in a white gown walked out into the waiting room, chart in hand, and called out Nana's name. While I fumbled to collect myself Nana had already disappeared inside, but a few moments later I heard someone say, could the guardian come with me?, and was led behind the curtained area. In the darkened space I could see Nana lying on a bed in a gown. The front of her gown was undone to expose her belly, which, I now saw, did have a slight bump after all.

Heartless.

To have kept it from me until now. To have hidden it. And to turn me into the unfeeling big sister who hadn't had a clue, not in all this time. Oh, she's heartless, all right. These thoughts ran through my head as I sat there on the verge of tears. You have a bump, Nana, I said stupidly, but Nana answered, as bumps go, it's not even that big, you know, in an infuriatingly composed and grown-up voice.

Let's take a look then, the doctor said.

She squirted a clear gel-like liquid around Nana's belly button, and spread it over the belly with one hand while extending the other to hold the monitor in place. Here's a foot, she said. It's the left foot, all five toes intact. And this here's the forearm, see the bone?

See?, she asked, and I was doing my best to hold my head up towards the monitor and nod, yes, but I honestly had no idea what I was looking at or even if my gaze was directed the right way. The monitor by Nana's feet was a mass of black, with scattered white motes, blotched shadows of white and grey. Here's the hand, and here's the face, the doctor said, moving the cursor around.

The baby's hiding behind its arm, so I'm afraid I can't make out the features.

But you can't leave before getting a good look at the baby's face, not when you've come all this way, insisted the doctor. Several times she asked Nana to turn over. Nana simply answered, yes, and did as she was told. Suddenly I saw a nose, it was squashed and wide.

Oh, I exclaimed, and said the baby's face was all squashed.

Only because we're pressing on it like this. Don't ever call the baby ugly, the doctor warned me. Here's a heart vessel, she pointed to an attenuated lump that resembled a sweet potato. Atrium, ventricle, she continued as we whirred through four darkened chambers that were opening and closing in rapid succession. Listen to this, she said and turned up the volume of the sounds coming from the depth of those chambers.

Sshaa sshaa sshaa sshaa sshaa sshaa sshaa.

I'd been expecting a ta-dum ta-dum sound; instead we heard a loud sshaa sshaa sshaa.

Sshaa sshaa.

Sshaa sshaa.

Sshaa sshaa.

Sshaa sshaa.

Sounds busy in there, I thought.

And very intense.

I wonder, is the baby all right?

To be surrounded by that, all that cacophony echoing in such a tiny space, it's got to be hard on the baby. Not able to turn away, always caught in the din. How unbearably loud it must seem.

My thoughts were all jumbled up.

Can the baby hear us? I asked.

The doctor answered, of course, in a tone that implied I'd asked an obvious question.

That's why you mustn't call the baby ugly.

—

Sshaa.

Sshaa.

Sshaa sshaa.

Sshaa sshaa.

Sshaa sshaa.

The next day and the day after that, the sound was all I could think about.

Out of all the stages of life, humans must exert the most kinetic energy while in the womb.

You'd have to, wouldn't you, just so you can start forming and growing your eyes, kidneys, spleen, heart, and all the rest of your tiny organs in mere months, while ensuring they're durable enough to last you a lifetime.

Sshaa sshaa.

Sshaa sshaa.

Sshaa sshaa.

Sshaa sshaa.

It's no wonder humans only ever see things from their own point of view.

When I said this, Nana and Naghi looked at me as though they hadn't a clue what I was talking about.

It was Sunday night, and we were in the kitchen with bags of flour and breadcrumbs out, about to heat the oil – Naghi had turned up after closing shop with the remainder of the tofu he'd bought for the bar, suggesting we make tofu croquettes.

What's she on about, Nana and Naghi seemed to be saying with their looks.

I mean, when you think about it, since from the first moment we're made, or that we start making our-selves, we do so while listening to our own sounds, I elaborated. The sshaa sshaa sshaa that flows from the heart and out to every other body part.

Isn't it ta-dum ta-dum? Naghi asked.

I shook my head. It's sshaa sshaa sshaa.

Whoosh sshaa sshaa?

It was more like sshaa sshaa sshaa.

It was a blood vessel, that's why, Nana said. She dipped the batter-coated chopsticks in the still-lukewarm oil.

What you heard was the sound of heart vessels.

Well, now that I've heard it, I can't seem to unhear it, I said.

That's different, though, Naghi interjected, even as his hands continued to dip the diced tofu in batter and bread them.

If you can't unhear it, that's probably because it's your own body you're hearing.

Well, my point is that we're all formed with this sshaa sshaa sshaa sound constantly in the background. With only that and nothing else filling up the entire space.

Probably there're other sounds, too.

Like what?

Sounds the mother's body is making, and sounds from outside. A person's belly is probably not entirely soundproof.

Is that so, I said.

So they say, Nana said.

Then I suppose it's so?, Naghi said.

Still, it's got to be noisy in there. Sshaa sshaa sshaa – not unlike cicadas, actually, I added.

Maybe next time I'll go and have a listen too, Naghi said casually, his eyes on the oil. The breaded tofu pieces rushed to the surface almost as soon as they were dropped in oil. Naghi stood by with long chopsticks in hand and fished them out as they did, and Nana received the cooked tofu on a serving dish and arranged them into a neat stack. The rows of croquettes soon formed a pyramid, and we sat down to eat, serving ourselves from the plate. But after one or two croquettes we found that this being anju, after all, we couldn't resist despite it being a Sunday night and got a few beers from the fridge. Naghi and I drank the beer while Nana sipped a tisane of persimmon leaf. From time to time I picked up a few croquettes and put them on Nana's plate. I noticed brown patches under Nana's downcast eyes as she sat quietly eating. But then she picked up the tofu I'd given her and moved them back onto the serving plate.

Whenever the time is right, she said, when I bring my boyfriend round, would you make these again for me?

Would you, together?

—

Listen, Aeja would say each time she phoned, which was about every three or four days.

I've started doing crafts.

What kind?

Paper.

Paper?

Paper-folding and crafts.

We don't use scissors, she added. She explained that the instructor brought pre-cut paper so scissors wouldn't be needed. With these they would fold cranes and balloons and flowers of various colours. Yesterday I made seven peonies, she told me now. I used glue to stick them together.

Did you?

Over the phone I could hear noises in the background that went something like gee gee or chi chi, sometimes saar saar. Each time she called, I would find myself listening to these sounds, trying to work out where she was phoning from. Somewhere out in the open air, maybe, gazing at or with her back turned to the sunlit brick wall. The green of the bamboo forest, the dusky depths of the pond. Chi chi, saar saar. Each time we spoke, I wondered whether I should bring up Nana and her news, but those muffled sounds over the phone like the audible vibrations of frail wings rubbing against each other stopped my mouth, and each time I'd hang up without having said anything of note.

———

Sora-ya.

Sora-ya, I heard the voice say, but I couldn't figure

out whose voice it was.

It had been an age since Aeja had called me by name, but even so I wondered if it wasn't Aeja on the other phone.

It's your baekmo, your father's older brother's wife.

Only then did I realise it wasn't Aeja. It's uncanny, I thought. Now that I know it isn't her, I don't see how I could have thought it was in the first place. When they don't sound anything alike, in either diction or voice. Baekmo, I repeated to myself, and an image of pinned-up hair, reddened forehead, and eyes that stared out at you from under scant eyebrows rose up in front of me.

Hello, Baekmo, I mumbled in greeting.

Your grandmother's birthday is coming up, she said, getting straight to the point.

This was, again, so completely out of the blue that I remained silent. Since Geumju ssi's death, Aeja, Nana, and I had not once attended any such family gathering. We didn't think to go ourselves, nor had anyone ever reached out to us with an invitation.

Be that as it may, my aunt said. And who was it, hmmm, that decided not one of you would so much as show your face, not once in all the years, she added in a reproachful tone. Well, this year your grandmother is insisting that she see you.

She explained that they were planning to drive to the outskirts for a health-boosting meal and invited Nana and me to join them. Not a word was said about Aeja. Bring Nana with you, she repeated. I replied that I would ask Nana, although I thought it unlikely that she'd agree to go.

She must be nearing her end, your grandmother, you won't believe how stubborn she's being, my uncle's wife remarked before ending the call.

———

I'd thought Nana would flatly refuse, but to my surprise she readily agreed to go.

What did they say was on the menu?

Duck, I said, and Nana replied, that sounds good, let's go have some duck.

The following Sunday I set out with Nana. Everyone was to gather at Baekmo's house from where a van would take us to the duck restaurant just outside the city. From where Nana and I lived it was a half-hour subway ride away. After three stations the subway made its way overground and continued on at ground level for some time. Through the windows the midday sun flooded in and rushed over the carriage floor, heating up Nana's and my feet. Nana was smartly attired in a flower-print dress and wore just enough makeup to keep her clear complexion intact.

I'd expected to see Father's other siblings along with a good number of relatives at this family gathering, but when we arrived, only my uncle and his wife, their son and daughter, and our grandmother – in short, her oldest son's family – were present. We were led into the living room, which boasted a fancy floral centrepiece, for a long overdue face-to-face with the family. Our grandmother appeared much older than I remembered. The feisty woman I'd seen at Geumju ssi's wake, the one who'd beat her fists on Aeja's back for spiriting her son away, was gone, replaced by an old woman with hardened features who sat a distance apart from the rest of the family. For someone who'd been adamant to see us she didn't seem at all eager to display any such feelings towards us now, and I had to wonder if her supposed insistence hadn't been a ruse set up by our uncle's wife.

The cousins were genial, all smiles and addressing us familiarly as older sisters, Nuna and Unni, as if the last time they'd set eyes on us they hadn't been mere toddlers of three or four and we'd been in regular contact all along. Meanwhile my eldest uncle and his wife, Baekbu and Baekmo, appeared the very embodiments of the breezy middle-class, demonstrating the relaxed parental attitudes of those who've attained a measure of comfort in life. Amid this light-hearted atmosphere of gentle chiding and playful evasions, Nana and I sat in silence, not having anything in particular to contribute.

I, for one, was feeling intimidated by the cousins' carefree attitudes. If they're a study in watercolour, Nana and I are sketches done with soy sauce, I thought to myself in stony silence, then felt repelled by the thought and repelled by myself for thinking it. Nana sat next to me with her back tensed and straight, looking just as uncomfortable. Clearly there were fault lines at work here, implicit as they may be, and when we eventually climbed into our uncle's van it was as the happy and harmonious on the one hand and the discordant who didn't know how to chime in on the other, with the silent, inscrutable old woman glaring at one then the other for reasons I couldn't fathom. Husband and wife sat up front in the driver's and passenger's seats, Nana and I took our places in the row behind them, and our grandmother sat alone in the next row while the two cousins took up the rear seats. Uncle kept on calling his wife older sister, Nuna, as if out of habit. Each time he did this Nana poked me in the ribs, and I'd poke her back, too, from time to time as the van bore us out of the city.

As we drove, Baekmo spoke at length about the

benefits of duck meat, how great it was for health, especially in the elderly. She'd like nothing better than to treat the elders in her side of the family to it, and generously too; what a pity it was that their circumstances didn't allow this. Today was an exception in light of it being Grandmother's birthday, may she enjoy the meal and keep in good health – in fact, one of her elderly kin had recently passed, but hadn't shown any sign of frailty. Quite on the contrary, this person had shown their usual appetite on the morning of the day and had then quietly slipped away later that same evening, and wasn't that a propitious death, that's how a person was meant to go after all, she brazenly continued. Grandmother didn't breathe a word through this unbroken monologue, and eventually the topic moved on to the two cousins messing around in the backseat. It turned out that the girl would be leaving home shortly to study abroad on a scholarship.

And what about you, Nana and Sora, have you got yourselves a man?, Baekmo lobbed at us all of a sudden.

When are the two of you planning on getting married?

It's best not to dilly-dally when it comes to marriage and family planning, she continued. You haven't a day to waste. All these problems these days, with low birth rates and what have you, they're only undermining our national power, the truth is there's no better way of being a patriot, she concluded with a peculiar logic I couldn't make heads or tails of. While her self-assured monologue continued, the rest of us sat in silence, remaining impassive. From where I was I could only see the back of Baekmo's head, and couldn't begin to imagine what expression she wore on her face as she spoke. A butterfly-shaped pin held her twisted-up hair in place. The butterfly's thorax was set in turquoise. Looking at it I suddenly recalled her wearing something similar in her hair all those years ago, at the wake.

It came back, unbidden: Baekmo and Baekbu had been among the relatives who put affairs in order after Geumju ssi's death.

Once resurfaced, the memory flooded back: the sight of Aeja lying as though dead in the master bedroom; Geumju ssi's brothers and co-workers squabbling in the living room, the latter saying the machinery had been turned off then restarted without warning, that was what had led to his death, the company's negligence was what was at fault here and therefore the proper thing would be for the company to take responsibility, that this incident must become the cornerstone of their struggle against dismal labour conditions – at which Geumju ssi's brothers demanded with raised voices: who do you see left in this household who can step up to that fight, we've no interest in fighting, we're up to our necks trying to scrape a living. These were the people who'd squared off against the workmates in suits when they came to pay their respects, these relations of ours who had taken it upon themselves to debate the details of the financial settlement and had then divvied up the payment among them. Through it all Aeja had remained bedridden, lying in utter stillness as if to hear the sound of her own breathing, while Nana and I kept close by, quelled into silence by the grown-ups around us.

The van made a sweeping right turn and pulled up at our destination. The duck restaurant sat off a major road amid tender green paddy fields of rice. It had been converted out of an old tile-roofed house with an adjoining yard. We had to wait our turn behind a queue of people who had also come to feast on duck meat. Someone from the restaurant told us there was a backyard we could stroll around in while we waited, and we set off round the corner as we'd been instructed. On top of some stone steps – a pile of sharp, jagged rocks that looked shoddily cut if not hacked – was a pavilion surrounded by a smattering of royal azaleas.

Let's sit in the shade out of this heat, Baekmo suggested.

Nana was sweating quite profusely. I reached out a hand to wipe the sweat from her brows but she shook her head as if to ward it off. We sat on chairs arranged in a circle under the hexagonal pavilion roof, our feet pointing towards one another. A long silence followed.

All grown up, Baekmo finally said in a tired tone directed at Nana and me.

So grown, I barely recognise you; in the street I'd have passed right by. Still: family's family. If any one of us here dies, we're the ones who'll come together at the end of the day.

She continued somewhat desultorily in this vein until someone came to say our table was ready. The stone steps were mossy and uneven in height; you had to watch where you trod. I held out a hand for Nana to take, but she lightly pushed it away and toddled down on her own.

We sat at the grease-stained floor table and waited for the duck. The table was actually a split log, it looked sufficiently heavy to pin down one's feet, and the dark scaly bark remained intact on its underbelly. Soon numerous small plates of side dishes were being laid out, nearly obscuring the table, and then the herb-fed duck was brought out. Having seated Grandmother at one end of the table, seeing as it was her birthday, Baekbu and his wife took up the middle seats and busied themselves with the portioning out of the meat and animated talk about the quality of the food. I picked up a piece of duck meat from the dish closest to me and placed it on Nana's plate. Nana dipped the meat in mustard sauce and started eating. Apart from Grandmother, the rest of Baekbu's family were busy discussing my cousin's upcoming departure. While they debated safety and exchange rates, heat and humidity levels over there, Nana and I kept quiet and concentrated on the food. Now and then I refilled Nana's plate with meat, and was about to give her some dressed scallions when I felt her cold hand grip my own under the table.

That's enough, she said in a whisper.

Enough.

This one here, his nickname's Abdul, actually, Baekmo was saying with a finger pointed at my cousin.

He takes after his father, has the same well-defined features as those Middle Easterners, so we call him Abdul.

The meal finished, so was the family outing, but it was already close to dusk by the time we headed back for the city.

That was a rare treat, Uncle smacked his lips with satisfaction.

Next to him sat Baekmo, with Grandmother in the row behind, Nana and I in the row behind that, followed by the two cousins in the rear, as before. There were a lot of cars making their way in from the outskirts and progress was slow. The van crept along in stops and starts while the setting sun cast the last of its burning rays into the car. It was peaceful and quiet now, unlike the drive out, the cousins and Baekmo and Grandmother drowsy with the glut of greasy food. Uncle had switched the radio on and an R&B singer crooned 'Moon River' set to an R&B rhythm. From my air-conditioned seat, the amber incandescence outside the window looked oddly unreal. Soon the day would set in a dusky pink glow. I was tired. Nana was asleep with her head resting awkwardly on one side. The makeup around her chin had faded, as though she'd dabbed at it a few too many times during dinner. I closed my eyes and was starting to nod off when I heard a dull voice say, you. When I opened my eyes, Grandmother was looking over her shoulder at me. She said nothing for the longest time and I started wondering if I hadn't dreamt it after all – when she finally spoke.

Nana looks a lot like Geumju when she's asleep.

This I hadn't expected – that I'd hear Geumju ssi's name. I was at a loss for words.

Geumju ssi: that is of course Geumju ssi's name. Nana and I and Aeja all call him Geumju ssi. But to hear it on someone else's lips – it made the name strange, unfamiliar. I felt ambushed. And then, too, to realise that there was a person out there who could call Geumju ssi, simply, Geumju.

Surely not many of those left in the world.

I looked at the aged face in front of me. Grandmother opened and shut her wrinkled eyelids before facing forward in her seat again. Nana let out a deep sigh in her sleep.

———

Don't.

This was the gist of the argument that night with Nana.

Don't do this, Nana kept saying as she paced about the room.

This is why I didn't tell you, because I was afraid you'd do this.

Do what?

This.

But what did I do?

Looking after me, and trying to be kind.

I can't be kind?

You don't want to though, do you?

How would you know? How would you know whether I wanted to be kind or not?

Of course I know. I know you, Unni. You're not happy about this. You're not. You hate this, that's the truth, so don't pretend, like I'm some poor pregnant woman you need to pity, don't do that to me.

But I'm not.

You are.

I resent it, Nana said. Being all considerate when you hate that I'm pregnant, it's revolting and I hate it.

I gaped at Nana, dumbstruck, like I'd received a blow to the head. I couldn't understand what I'd just heard. Nana continued to pace the room, her eyes glued to the floor, lost in her own thoughts. She'd complained of indigestion earlier and kept wringing the flesh between her thumb and forefinger, hoping for relief. The root of her thumb was already quite red.

What is it I've done exactly, I demanded. I was rigid, my body taut to the point of trembling, the words came out mangled as though I'd chewed through my own tongue.

I'm only trying to look out for you because I'm

worried.

So don't.

What's that supposed to mean.

What I just said. Leave me be. You resent it, fine, so leave me be. Or be honest about it and say you resent it. If you can't come out and say it, then leave me be. Don't lie and pretend to be kind. Don't try and take care of me.

It's exactly like before, she said, you mean to repeat the whole thing again.

I had no idea what she meant by before and cast about, dumbly, trying to figure out when or what she was referring to.

Like when we were kids, Nana spat out.

Like those kids did back then, when you and I went back to school after Geumju ssi's funeral, when they tried so hard to be nice to us. Do you know what that was? They were being kind out of *pity*. They *pitied* us, and they were scared too, of course, but then none of it really concerned them either, that's why – that's why they kept watching you and me, from their safe distance, from just far enough away that they could afford to be nice. And that's exactly what you're doing to me, Unni. You won't say how you really feel and you won't argue with me. Don't you think I know, though? I know, Unni. I know you find it a nuisance. I know you resent me. I know you're always wishing I wasn't here, that it'd be better if I wasn't. And still you fake kindness, hiding your resentment and pretending to look out for me.

Nana stopped where she was and slumped to the floor.

You keep doing that, and it makes me feel so helpless...

As if there's no one else in the world but me – and then I feel so unbearably lonely.

—

Bitch.

I thought.

Bitch.

I repeated over and over in my head.

Revolting?

Of course, she'll call me Unni then, and not Sora.

Then she calls me Unni.

Only then.

The cold front lingered for days.

Nana was distant. So distant in fact that she seemed a different person altogether, if not an entirely different species of being. I'd always thought us inseparable, seeing how there'd only ever been the two of us, but now, as if overnight, I'd become someone who revolted her. Or maybe it hadn't happened overnight, to think so was perhaps pure vanity – at this thought, my lips immediately sealed themselves shut. She must have thought it often enough for the word to have left *her* lips so matter-of-factly. I may be the one who'd been called revolting, but to come out with *that*, and all because I'd shown some kindness, well, that made Nana the truly revolting one, I thought – or tried to think.

I resent it.

I do.

But I don't have a choice, do I?

Since you're my baby sister.

And that can't be undone.

Several times a day I had to tamp these words back down, stop myself from hurling them at the back of her head, and the effort alone made my face flush scarlet three or four times a day.

Over time I could tell that the strain on her body was increasing. She was finding it harder to wake herself up in the morning and each time I saw her seated at the front door putting on her shoes, her hair flat on the crown of her head, I felt sorry for her. Then the word *revolting* would float back up, and immediately the pit of my stomach would grow cold. Nana and I did our best to avoid running into each other by adjusting our daily schedules and outings. When we both happened to be at home, we gave each other a wide berth, as though we were magnets of the same charge. Stifling heat or not, we each lay low behind our own shuttered doors: when one door clicked open, the other would click shut; when this door closed, the sound of the other being opened would soon follow. When I needed to use the bathroom or the living room, I would stand behind my door and listen for any hint of movement outside. It was awkward and tiresome to live like this in an already cramped house, but this only made my resolve harden.

Bitch.

I'd repeat to myself.

—

Then, on one of those nights, I had a dream.

Nana and I both appeared in the dream. We had shrunk to mushroom proportions and were standing at the roadside of a busy thoroughfare. While gigantic feet landed all around us, the thuds as deafening as falling bombs, Nana and I were somehow holding on, managing to avoid being trampled on. We each had a shovel in hand. When I glanced at my feet, I saw that we were standing inside a circle drawn in the dirt.

Okay, we start digging now, I told Nana, and

struck the ground beneath me.

Nana thrust her shovel into the earth alongside me. Now we've begun, I thought to myself, only to find myself, the next moment, inside the very pit I'd dug. I raised my head and looked up. I could see the outline of the hole, the soil I'd dug up in a mound alongside it. Clouds dotted the sky like shredded cotton. Perhaps Nana was still at it – the sound of earth being scooped up could be heard at regular intervals. It went rasp-thud, rasp-thud. I remained standing there with my face lifted towards the edge of the pit, when the sound stopped.

Unni, I heard the thin wail of someone calling.

I was shouting, Nana-ya, in answer to it when the curtain brushed my face and prompted me to open my eyes.

The rasp-thud I'd thought I heard must have been the sound of the curtain grazing my face. I'd been sleeping with my head towards the window of late, hoping it would make the oppressive night-heat more bearable. The fan churned, looking listless after a night of hard work. I got out of bed thinking I might indeed have called out to Nana in my sleep. I'd over-slept without meaning to, it being a weekend.

Out in the living room Nana was drinking a tall glass of milk. I headed for the fridge as though I hadn't seen her and reached for the carafe of water. I was just about to pour myself a glass, when I felt a trembling in the air. The walls and the floor were shaking too, ever so slightly. I went to the window and looked outside. There was a car parked outside at street level with the engine idling. Its silver body shimmered brightly in the baking heat. Behind the sealed windows, in the car's doubtless cool interior, sat a figure with both arms on the wheel as though waiting for someone. A sudden gust of hot air climbed the wall and rushed at me through the living room window. The wind chime tinkled, and then I heard Nana pad over to her room and click the door shut behind her.

It was too stifling and awkward to remain at home, so I put on my trainers and went out for a stroll. I wandered towards the subway station, then went ahead and got on the subway and rode the two stops to the riverside park. The park was teeming with people basking in the fair weather on their day off. I sat on the hot grass and watched people pass by on inline skates and bicycles, or with their dogs. Afterwards I got on the subway in the direction home, then thought I might as well continue past my stop; eventually I transferred to a line that would take me to the care home where Aeja was. It being a spur-of-the-moment trip, I was dressed in gym clothes and ratty trainers. I didn't have a bag or anything, all I had was a single credit card. After stepping off the subway, I had to stand for twenty minutes under the awning of a sweltering bus stop besieged by blistering sunrays and swirling dust clouds, before the bus finally trundled to a stop.

On the fringes of the hill leading up to the home, I could see scarlet sage and zinnias in bloom. The lotus-laden pond was thick and oozing the boggy odour of water. Beyond, the bamboo forest barely stirred.

At the reception window there was a casebound spiral notebook for visitors.

I grabbed the biro, which was fixed to the counter with a rubber band, and wrote down Aeja's name followed by my own on the visitors' list.

Aeja didn't seem particularly glad to see me, greeting me almost indifferently.

I found her in the crafts room where radio music was playing and where she had been making blossoms out of paper that had been pre-cut into oval shapes.

She dug out a small bottle of drinking yoghurt from her pocket, saying she'd saved it from snack time a half-hour earlier. I could feel Aeja's body heat on it. I pressed my thumbs into the foil lid covering the mouth of the bottle to make two small holes, put the bottle to my mouth and drank out of one of the holes. This allows the yoghurt to flow out smoothly. A trick I'd learned from Nana.

Of course.

I learned it from Nana, didn't I, I thought dumbly.

—

Listen,

Aeja said to me.

I heard a story from this woman who's new downstairs.

There was this married couple, see.

In the village where she lived as a girl, there was this perfectly matched happy young couple.

But being as happy as they were, they naturally aroused the envy of a ghost.

And one day the husband was swept away by the rain floods as he was walking home.

The villagers found only his umbrella, adrift in the torrent downstream.

But the wife refused to believe it.

She was sure her husband was alive somewhere, all summer and autumn she walked along that stream, calling his name.

Until the village people took pity on the wife and took to going round hers to light the fire pit in her kitchen every night.

Then one day, the wife, who'd been staring at the flames burning in the agung'i from the kitchen doorway, suddenly burst out laughing.

And when whoever had been tending to the fire briefly left the kitchen and returned a short while later, it was to find that the wife had crawled into the burning pit.

But her expression and her skin in that fiery blaze, nothing could have been more beautiful, that's what she says.

Beautiful, she said.

I couldn't do it though, what the wife did, that's how I ended up this unbeautiful thing.

That's not true, I said. You're still pretty.

That's not what I'm saying, is it, Aeja sighed, and with a rustle resumed her folding.

The radio time bulletin announced five o'clock.

NANA

▬▬▬

娜 娜

Nana here.

    I'll begin.

—

Nana is 娜娜, the first and last characters being identical.

    Na repeated twice to form Na-na, which even in reverse means one thing: beautiful. This name is bound to be, at a probability of eight out of nine, Aeja's handiwork. Typical Aeja, Sora would say, whereas I, the actual bearer of the name, find her imprint excessive: it's a name with a disproportionately high Aeja content.

    Still, the symmetry of it does resonate, and na being a homonym for na, that is, I, there's of course an extra phonetic echo, so that Nana and na start to merge, become interchangeable. Whether I say Nana or na, I mean myself.

In fact, Nana is a good name to say out loud. Compared to a Soyeon or a Yeonsook, compared to starting every sentence with Soyeon this or Yeonsook that, Nana is a lot easier to say, it glides right off the tongue. Sometimes I refer to myself as Nana. Only people with an inflated ego call themselves by their own name, I've been told in one standoffish tone or another. But as far as Nana's concerned, anyone who finds that much surplus ego offensive enough to point out, is bound to have an inflated sense of self, too. I am Nana. Nana is me. And Nana finds that the list of things about which she feels indifferent outruns the tally of her likes and dislikes. Liking, disliking: either way, one is bound to have to commit, to exert an effort. Better, then, to steer clear and remain ambivalent. And there are plenty of things Nana's decided she's indifferent about. Nana's indifferent to peaches. Nana's indifferent to apples. She's indifferent to winter and to snow. Nor does she care one way or the other for rain, or cats, or dogs, or owls. Since a young age, Nana's been indifferent to adults, as she has been to children. And this remains true to this day, despite the fact that Nana is, at present, pregnant.

Pregnant: a pregnant woman, an imsanbu. That's

a strangely awkward word, imsanbu, it trips up the tongue. The bu 婦 in imsanbu means wife or daughter-in-law. Nana is neither of these things, for the moment; all she is is Nana, which may be why the term sits so strangely in the mouth. Imsanbu: if said enough times would it start to feel familiar? What if one were to write it down over and over again, imsanbu imsanbu imsanbu. No, it's no use. Despite how she may appear to the world, Nana feels extremely out of her depth right now. She feels awkward and apprehensive – and guarded. And when Nana's feeling guarded, Nana refers to herself in the third person. She does this when she's feeling lonely, too. The more alone and anxious Nana feels, the more frequently Nana supplants I, until it's all Nana this, Nana that, Nana Nana all the time. The person who gave Nana her name, Aeja, was someone who, true to her own name, once brimmed with love, was nothing if not love. And so upon losing that love, she ended up a curious thing: she ended up a mere empty husk.

—

One day, back when our father Geumju ssi was alive, I came upon the strangest thing.

It's unclear exactly when this took place, but it was

the same year that Aeja, who had grown up an orphan,
decided to offer jesa to her parents. I seem to recall it
as summer – it was around then Aeja spoke of someone appearing in her dreams. It wasn't anyone she
knew, but this strange figure would randomly mate-
rialise in front of her and sit quietly by her side as she
lay tucked under her blankets, or moan loudly, or ask
indecipherable questions such as, do you like fa or sol.
The one thing which was clear was that this person
was quite dead. This is no ordinary dream, Aeja said
finally, and went to see a diviner. When she returned
she related what she'd been told, her face wearing its
usual expression: one of her parents had passed away
some time ago and this was who kept dropping by,
the reason for the visitations being that the spirit –
not having received a jesa table – was thirsty. The
jesa table that promptly materialised was small and set
out in the room shared by Aeja and Geumju ssi. Two
vertical strips of paper inked with Hanja characters
were taped on the wall, and plates of rice cake, pears,
and bowls of grain alcohol laid out directly beneath
these. Geumju ssi went first, kneeling in front of the
low table before bowing deep and flat so his forehead touched his gathered hands on the floor. The
jibang was written in Geumju ssi's handwriting, the
paper undulant beneath the ink-soaked brushstrokes.

What do the wavy squiggles that look like ghosts say, I asked, and Geumju ssi read out the characters for me: Hyeongo Haksaeng Bugoon Shinwi, Hyeonbi Yu'in Mo-ssi Shinwi, the spiritual bodies of Respected Father and Respected Wife from Family X. The one on the left is for Nana's grandfather, the right-hand one for Nana's grandmother, he added. It's not quite proper to offer jesa to both elders as one is still living, but since we don't know which of them has passed, I've gone ahead and written both names down. Then Sora and I made our bows, deep and low and flat on the floor just as Geumju ssi had taught us to, and then it was Aeja's turn. After her second bow she didn't rise, but remained prostrate. She made no move to get up or alter her pose, the whites of her soles showing under her buttocks, and this continued for such a long time that Sora and I started to fidget with worry, but Geumju ssi let her be.

I remember it as the fifteenth day of the lunar month.

Once we were all done bowing we left the room so the ancestors could have their meal in peace, and sat round the living room to eat watermelon. Aeja was her usual self as she carefully split the fruit open, cutting the unwieldy pieces into easily manageable slices. The red flesh revealed by Aeja's knife spread out evenly right to the edge, fully ripe and sweet. Sora and I scrambled to get our hands on the tastiest middle parts, and before long I was stuffed and left the three seated round the table to go and pee. On the way to the bathroom I noticed that the door of the room where the jesa table was laid out was slightly ajar. Without much thought, I peered through the crack that was about two finger joints wide, and amid the smell of candle wax and flame and the subtle scent of Chinese ink, I saw a hand reach out and grab a pear from a plate. All this happened in the blink of an eye; I barely had time to register any details about the hand. Someone's there, I thought, as I backed away from the door. Then I headed to the bathroom, peed, and returned to the living room for more watermelon. I didn't understand what I'd witnessed, and soon forgot what I'd glimpsed through the gap. It wasn't a secret so much as I was merely the only one who knew about the incident, having so promptly erased it from my mind.

It wasn't until this morning that I dreamt of that someone – the person belonging to that hand.

I'd opened my eyes to find the room sunk in darkness, a large window by my head. I knew it was a dream by the size of that window; the window in my room is nowhere as big. Outside the window there was a staircase that ascended to the right, and an old woman I'd never seen before sat stooped on it, peering into my room. There seemed to be a bluish light coming from somewhere above us; the top of her head with its scant hair and her rounded shoulders were bathed in it as she sat unmoving and silent. She gazed at the room with a sorrowful air, before slowly gathering her shadowed lips together to form the words, where is Aeja. When I answered that Aeja was at a care home, she grew mournful and muttered to me to go get her. This must be the person to whom that hand belonged, I told myself in the dream. The hand Nana had seen and been so quick to forget all those years ago, it belonged to this woman – to Grandmother – this must be Aeja's mother.

Mustn't it?

I wanted to ask Sora, wanted to tell her about the dream and see if she agreed with me, but I couldn't. These days Sora and Nana are barely talking to each other. Sora's not speaking to Nana as much as Nana is not speaking to Sora. It's debatable which of the two is less eager to engage with the other. To be fair, I did, in retrospect, speak harshly. I did call her revolting, after all. The stunned look on Sora's face. She'd turned as pale as a sheet, but I figure she must have had a reason to be shocked since why else would the blood have run out of her so? I'd touched a nerve, that's why she took it so hard; that's what Nana thinks, to be honest. Sora's sly. Sora's delicate. She's sly, to be so delicate. A body that's soon to become a mother – I know she finds that a chilling prospect, I know she resents the idea of a baby, and still she won't let up on the niceness, the kind, thoughtful gestures. She's behaving no differently than anyone else, from how the rest of them would be behaving in these circumstances. She's acting as she might have seen people do on television, being caring and supportive when her heart or whatever is not in the least in it.

What a mess.

There are times when Sora fails to see Aeja.

It's difficult to say when this started, this unseeing, since I myself only gradually became aware of it. Sora would stop short, finally realising that Aeja had been there, right next to us all along, and exclaim, oh, you gave me such a fright. It was quite funny at first, we used to laugh about it, but after a while it reached a point where I couldn't laugh it away any more. This was about three years ago, I think.

That year I'd come down with a severe flu as autumn lapsed into winter, and for four consecutive days I'd had to take time off from work. The fever would rage then settle, then rage again, I was shivering constantly, I ached all over, my body felt like a soggy, formless, sweating heap. The persistent fever seemed to alarm even Aeja, and she had spent that particular day by my side. Sora came home from work as usual in the evening and plopped down on the floor by my blankets to ask how I was feeling, then rummaged around in her bag and pulled out a banana pudding. It was from the neighbourhood patisserie, this yellow pudding in a plastic cup. It was the closest thing to an honest banana flavour and we used to buy it regularly. Sora stretched out her stockinged legs, dusty from the day, dug out three puddings and placed them on her skirt. After ripping the lids off, she placed one in my hand along with a disposable spoon, put one down by her side saying, this one's Aeja's, then picked up the third and began scooping it with her spoon. She ate it the way she eats everything: fastidiously, gazing intently at the opaque yellow surface of it all the while, ruminating over each bite. I watched her with my fever-dimmed eyes. I told her to give one to Aeja, too. Sora took another bite of the pudding before saying, she wasn't in her room.

But she's right here.

At this Sora's eyes bulged, she looked about the room with the spoon still in her mouth. Aeja was seated by my side, near the foot of where I lay, as she had been all this time. But Sora made as if she still couldn't see her, gaping in confusion even as her eyes roved in Aeja's direction. From the edge of my blanket Aeja looked on dispassionately, not uttering a word as Sora continued to fail to see her. To my fevered, tearful eyes both of them appeared, in that moment, equally horrifying.

—

It's possible that Aeja doesn't care one way or the other if she's visible to other people or not.

Whether they can see her or not.

Why would it.

She may have been long dead by that point, or as good as dead.

She'd tried to kill herself, hadn't she, all those years ago.

—

Sora was eleven, I was ten, and we had just packed up and left the house we'd lived in with Geumju ssi. The moment we arrived at the new house, Sora and I had stepped out again to return the handcart we'd borrowed as Aeja had asked us to do. The rag man's cart was old and worn, its bottom fixed up with multiple patches and bits of plywood, and there were a few stumped remnants of knotted cords that must have proved impossible to undo. The handle was wound with worn-out elastic cord and soft to the touch. At first the two of us stood side by side and heaved the handle together, nearly hanging off of it at times as we dragged the cart behind us. Later, we came up with a game where we would take turns to ride the cart while the other pulled. Every thirty steps we'd change places and hence change our role in the story. This was the rule, and we stuck to it as we alternately pushed and rode until our foreheads and temples were dewy with sweat. After thirty steps, when it became my turn to ride again, I would jump on the cart as quick as I could and huddle on my hands and knees. I'm the rabbit on the back of the sea turtle, being smuggled down to the palace of the sea king, I told myself.

And soon they'll have my liver, they'll make a meal of it.

But the turtle's too quick, I can't possibly get off now.

It's all very unfair.

They'll tear out my liver, they'll gobble it up, I'd repeat to myself, and the thought would make me so sad I'd cower in the cart, eyes watering, until it came time to switch places so that now I was the turtle, meaning I was in the position to demand the rabbit's liver, and I would forge ahead boldly with the cart.

Rabbit, rabbit, give me your liver, your liver will cure our sea king, so give it up, give up that liver of yours.

Eventually the game brought us to our old house, and we saw with astonishment that the front door was open. There was a man inside, he was wearing strange pants that reached up to his chest, and he had a dirty hat on. Sora tensed immediately. Her lips pursed shut and the back of her sweaty neck stiffened with anxiety. The man was pawing through our plates and kitchenware, and even after he'd spotted us, he seemed unfazed. Instead he carried on looting our rice bowls and our spoons, the stuff that belonged to us, to our home. I was nervous by now and clung to Sora's arm, begging to leave, but Sora crept inside as if possessed. When she re-emerged she looked very pale. As soon as we'd turned our backs on the house, Sora set off at a rapid pace. Quickly, quickly, she urged me – she was half running now. I couldn't keep up with her. I moved my legs as best I could, eyes glued to the back of her head, but I was lagging behind. I kept lagging, Nana kept lagging, Nana, then I, both lagging, both falling behind, and now Nana feels – entirely alone. Nana's legs may well be planks now, with each step forward it feels like she'll topple over, and the moment she does she's bound to be left behind, and this is too frightening a thought, she's terrified to be left behind. Unni-ya, she calls desperately, but Sora doesn't look back, not once does she look back. Instead she presses on at the same speed, showing only the small back of her that seems to be pulsing with fear, crying out oh no, oh no, oh no in stricken silence.

Unni-ya.

Unni-ya.

Unni-ya, Nana keeps howling, and if she still doesn't look back then she's no big sister, Nana is thinking. Sora is what I'll call you, then. I'll never call you Unni ever again.

We arrived to find Aeja lying on the floor in exactly the same manner as when we'd left to return the cart. Sora kicked off her shoes the moment we entered the door, rushed to Aeja's side, and sank down next to her. Her shoulders heaving and lips clamped as though she were trying to control her breath, ragged from the tremendous speed at which we'd been walking, she glared at Aeja, hands clenched into two tight fists on her thighs. Strands of hair, slick with sweat, stuck fast to the nape of her neck. Then Nana caught the briny lukewarm smell wafting up from Sora, from where she stood looking at Aeja — and she knew. Just like that, Nana knew: Aeja had meant to die.

After sending Sora and Nana out on a chore, Aeja had meant to die.

Dead already.

Dead ten times, a hundred times over.

Laid out like that, ripped to a thousand shreds.

—

To know a thing like that, to realise it just like that — that was the kind of childhood Sora and I had.

But it's true that Sora and I also got to know Naghi Oraboni during that same period, so I couldn't say my impressions of that time are altogether horrifying either.

My father's dead, too, Naghi Oraboni told us one day.

After hearing his story I felt more at ease and dropped my guard around him. To think a story like that had a soothing effect on me, even inspired a special affinity, especially at that age — well, maybe I'm the creepy, repulsive one, not Sora, maybe I'd been the odd one, even as a child. In any case, this was around the time Sora and Naghi Oraboni turned twelve within three months of each other.

My father's dead, too, Oraboni told us.

I heard he collapsed one winter while moving apples. They saw him, the grown-ups at the market, they said he just keeled over as if he'd stumbled, and died on the spot. He couldn't move, the carrying rack and the apple crates had him pinioned to the ground, and the grown-ups didn't dare lay a finger on him in case his neck was broken. So he died where he lay. I heard that a lot of the market people came to the wake, but not one of them expressed sorrow at his death. Apparently he had quite the reputation for being this mild-mannered guy who'd do an about-face after a few drinks, start breaking things, and people. No wonder most of the guests weren't sad to see him gone, even though they pitied him his life – that's what my mother says. That it was fortunate he died. And is that why she cries at every jesa?, I'd like to know. If it's a good thing he's dead, why cry at all, I say.

This was the tale Naghi Oraboni told us one night. That day some of their relatives had come over for a small, quiet jesa ceremony, after which he'd crossed over to ours, looking quite hassled, with plates of rice cake and fritters. He talked and talked that night, and wouldn't stop stuffing himself with the food he'd supposedly brought round for us.

Aeja has never prepared a jesa table for Geumju ssi.

Right after moving into that peculiarly constructed house where we were to spend most of our childhood, Sora and I agreed that Geumju ssi should never go thirsty and got into the habit of leaving out a bowl of water by our heads every night. Each morning we measured how much water had disappeared overnight. If the dip was substantial Geumju ssi had been and gone, and if it wasn't he hadn't been very thirsty. Playing house meant only one thing to us then: pretending to hold a jesa for Geumju ssi.

Hyeongo Haksaeng Bugoon Shinwi.

Geumju ssi had explained these words to me once, and they'd left an impression on me ever since. You write it like this, I'd brag, and write out the words in pencil on thin exercise paper, over and over again. I was being a show-off, but I was also probably getting it wrong each time, scribbling Bugun Shinyi instead of Bugoon Shinwi, for example, and childishly believing I'd got it right. I wrote the characters – whatever they actually spelled – in Korean script, in Hangul, and not in Hanja as Geumju ssi had done. Still, Sora was sufficiently impressed with what I'd done. She'd choose the best version, where my handwriting was the neatest, and carefully tape it to the wall. This signalled that the jesa had begun. Sora and I were the chief mourners. Naghi Oraboni was assigned the role of the guest who'd come to give his condolences, and the jesa ceremony would begin with the receiving of this guest. We would light candles and place plates of caramels and breadcrumbs just below the name-papers I'd written out. Then Sora and I would sit and start keening, wailing aigo aigo, which was the cue for Naghi Oraboni to stand by the door for a moment, before stepping over the threshold to enter the room and pay his respects. After getting down on his knees and bowing, twice, he would turn to us and say, in a very mature and sincere manner, how great your sorrow must be. This was the proper order of play. And when we wanted to hold the jesa on a grander scale, whoever happened to be playing the guest had to back out of the room and step over the threshold again for as many times as was necessary, taking on the role of a different guest each time. There were occasions when we swapped roles, and would have Naghi Oraboni play chief mourner while Sora and I played guests, but the two of us could never outmatch him. Of the three of us he was easily the best guest, his was the most grown-up and natural delivery of those empathic words.

Once we'd run out of words to exchange and had our fill of lamenting, we'd sit down next to each other and watch the candles. We watched until the flames burned through the wax then subsided. Even at midday the room didn't see much natural light and remained cool and dim, flickering in the meagre but warming wax light. The room held us in that glow: our bodies, the low luminescence, and the room glinting, quivering, removed from the rest of the world.

After a while Sora suddenly spoke up, though her eyes remained on the elongated, shimmering shadow of the flame.

We'll do the same when Aeja's dead, we'll hold a jesa for her just like this one, she said.

I nodded and said nothing, even as I told myself, no, I won't ever do that. But this is a secret I keep to myself.

Even if she comes to me and pleads and begs, I won't spare her a bowl of water, I told myself – but these thoughts must remain, naturally, my secret.

—

I won't ever call her Unni again.

Despite my resolve, however, there have been moments when I find myself calling out Unni-ya, usually in moments of distress. Not that she's ever complained much when I call her by name. She'll feign annoyance from time to time, demanding, must you do that?, but it's not in earnest. When I call out Sora-ya, eight times out of ten she will turn to me. In fact Nana's willing to bet that Sora secretly prefers this. Because it's easier to just be Sora, isn't it, than to be the big sister? Sometimes I feel like needling her, but that would draw tears from Sora, she's bound to cry at that, and knowing this Nana just can't. Sora's sly. Sora's delicate. She's sly to be so delicate.

Aeja has shown little sign of dying since that day all those years ago.

No need, as she's as good as dead; instead, she'll occasionally cease all life-sustaining acts and fuck herself up, which fucks Sora up and fucks Nana up. Nana refuses to be party to any such thing ever again. So you see, Grandmother, showing up in my dreams and pleading with me to bring her back, well, it's never going to work.

My mind's made up.

Nana refuses to go through any of that ever again.

As you can see, I'd had valid reasons for deciding to send Aeja to a care home.

———

I'll go on.

The morning I'd been jolted out of sleep by that unsettling visit happened to be the morning of the day I'd promised to meet Moseh ssi's parents. This would be my first encounter with his parents, and my first time visiting his home. When I asked about them, Moseh ssi replied that they were ordinary: ordinary people, ordinary family.

Moseh ssi had arrived early and was waiting downstairs. I'd slept in that morning and only just got out of bed, I'd barely had time to look out the window, but I could tell he was there from the noise in the street: his engine was running. Holding the glass of milk in my hand, I headed to the window and looked down. To confirm that it is in fact his car, that it is his head I see. Yes, there he is: arms resting on the wheel, head cocked to one side above his hands, eyes fixed upstairs. Even when our eyes meet he doesn't stir, doesn't gesture as if to say come on then; instead he goes on watching. Why does he stare the way he does, I think to myself as I stare right back down at him. This happens all the time with him. One of us looks at the other, so the other looks back, looks because looked at, looks at the looking back, is looked back at so looks again – this relentless cycle repeating without end. Not a word is exchanged throughout, there's only the mutual staring that verges on glaring.

I had been in a few relationships before meeting Moseh ssi.

I was in fact with someone when I first started seeing him. This other person was a colleague at work, a large man, unlike Moseh ssi. And unlike the rest of my work colleagues, who were invariably listless, glum, and meek, this man was brazenly cheerful and upbeat, quick to laugh and to talk, his face a riot of expressions; and he was good with people. There was a tacit ban on workplace relationships, and I agreed with him to keep things quiet and dated him secretly for about six months. But this man, together with another colleague, had a habit of ambushing me whenever we were out as a group. We'd be out walking somewhere, perhaps on our way to a team dinner, and out of nowhere the pair of them would jump out at Nana. More likely than not I'd be lagging behind my colleagues, feeling drained and empty after an exhausting day, dragging my feet, when out of nowhere these two men would run up, yell right into my ears, and make their getaway. Waahh, they'd shout from either side of me, and the world around Nana's ears would crumple from the shock of it, I'd be stunned into place, completely disoriented, while the two men dashed ahead of me, laughing with glee. This happened again and again and again. Waahh, they'd yell, waahh! Waahh!

Waahh!

The last time it happened, I'd turned on my heels and promptly struck off in the opposite direction. This won't do, I thought to myself, feeling a sudden stinging in my eyes and nose.

Nana ssi, where are you going, he said when he'd finally caught up with me, but I brushed his hand off my arm as brusquely as I could and continued on my way.

Come on, you know it was only in fun, he whispered, afraid someone might hear.

At that I turned and gave him a look, before walking away. Click-clack, click-clack, I hurried on, fuming with outrage. How could he, when we'd said we'd keep it a secret, it's infuriating, I thought as I picked up my pace, but there was someone behind me, another colleague had followed and caught up with me. It was Moseh ssi.

It's time I got ready, I'll be late.

I'm debating whether or not to have another glass of milk when the door to Sora's room opens and she patters out. I thought she'd hurry right back in and close the door when she spotted me, as is the pattern these days, but for some reason she pretends to be half-asleep and pads right into the kitchen. She must have been sweating in her sleep, because I can hear her bare soles unsticking themselves from the floor with every step. She gets a glass of water, saunters over to the window, and looks out it in her dishevelled state. From where she's standing now it's likely she can see Moseh ssi's car and Moseh ssi himself. Moseh ssi may well still have his eyes trained on the window too. Before returning to my room and clicking the door shut, I consider saying, he's the baby's father, but we're not speaking at the moment, and Moseh ssi has been waiting long enough as it is. So I don't. I tell myself, maybe next time.

———

Moseh ssi doesn't eat strawberries.

He says he was taught that the skin is the filthiest part of any fruit. It was Moseh ssi's father who instilled this in him from an early age, and accordingly he eats only peeled fruit. Whether he's eating an apple or a peach or whatever else, he waits until his mother has removed the skin with a fruit knife, and only then eats the slices handed to him. Who knows what pesticides and other chemicals may have seeped through to the flesh, or what muck attached itself to the skin during picking. For these reasons grapes are strictly avoided, since with grapes one must suck the skin in order to get at the flesh inside, as are strawberries, which don't even possess outer layers to peel off. That's the family custom he was brought up to subscribe to, and although he himself wouldn't go so far as to say he dislikes strawberries or finds them unhygienic, in any case he finds he is not particularly inclined towards eating them. This is Moseh ssi's final word regarding his pickiness about strawberries. This – the fact that he has an aversion to strawberries – this is one of a number of peculiarities he shares, oddly enough, with Naghi Oraboni.

Then there are the ways in which they are entirely dissimilar. For instance, Moseh ssi's footsteps are utterly silent. This is extremely odd, both to discover and to observe. Once, after a date, I even failed to notice that he'd been shadowing me for all of twenty minutes since we'd said our goodbyes. Curious to see if his shoes had special leather or rubber soles that muffled his tread, I turned them over one day while he was asleep, but they were like any other pair with regular soles. The mouths of the shoes, where his feet fitted, were stretched slightly and had darkened from repeated friction. They were, in short, ordinary. Ordinary – there's a snail's shell of a thought that once traced will coil in on itself endlessly. Who knows, I'll sometimes tell myself, maybe it's this ordinariness that enables him to walk inaudibly in the first place. But whatever the case may be, the fact remains that Moseh ssi is the sort of person who is able to entirely silence his steps while wearing the most ordinary shoes, and this I find somewhat frightening, even if I can't quite explain the reasons why. But yes, I do find it a little alarming.

For a while, the man who used to scare Nana by jumping out of nowhere to yell in her ear appeared to be in a state of agony. But soon enough all trace of heartache vanished and he was back to his former self. Lately he's started dating someone else. They seem to have agreed to forgo the whole 'let's keep it between us' compact, they make no attempt to hide their intimacy or the fact that they are a couple. The man remains jovial, always quick to laugh and to speak out, and a deft hand at all aspects of work life. The soreness – not heartache as it turns out – he'd exhibited towards Nana is forgotten, and now they coexist as indifferent colleagues.

That had been the extent of their relationship.

When it comes to love, that seems about the right amount of emotional involvement: to be able to soon get back on your feet no matter what occurs. Where whether by mutual agreement or by one-sided betrayal or because one of you vanishes into thin air overnight, the other can manage to say, in due time: I'm fine. That seems about right. Even once the baby is here, Nana's decided that that will be the extent of her love for the child and for Moseh ssi.

Pouring all your heart into love as Aeja had done

– that level of devotion is what Nana wants to guard herself against.

—

There's a dreamcatcher hanging from the rear-view mirror of Moseh ssi's car. It resembles a circular spider's web. The round frame is made from bent animal bone, and within is a delicate webbing of wispy silver threads, a dainty bead barely the size of an adzuki bean nestled near its centre. Once, when I remarked that the bead looked like a prey caught in a spider's web, Moseh ssi told me it was in fact a dewdrop. Dreamcatchers filter out bad dreams and let only the good ones pass; the bad dreams remain tangled in the web for the night, and when daylight breaks they turn to dew and evaporate, he explained. The long feather that hangs from the circle flutters in the air as the car progresses in stops and starts and sweeping turns.

I'm looking at the bead in all that webbing when we arrive at the grounds of the apartment complex. The street runs in one direction between the several blocks of apartments, so if you were to take a wrong turn while driving you'd have to go round forever, trying to find your way out of the maze you'd gotten yourself into. So this is where Moseh ssi lives, I think to myself. We wait for the lift to arrive, get in, our footsteps echoing hollow on the metal floor, and ascend.

Welcome.

Moseh ssi's mother opens the door. Her bobbed hair has been set into voluminous curls, and her features are astonishingly pronounced. Her eyelids are overly wrinkled from years of applying makeup with a heavy hand, and today they're covered in a darkish shade, while her rouged lips are pink and smooth and glossy. Nana registers the sharp sidelong glance Moseh ssi's mother darts at her belly while welcoming her in. And the man with the air of a retired army general, who's sporting a vest in this heat, is Moseh ssi's father. As soon as Nana removes her shoes and steps up to the hallway, he offers her a hand, says, nice to meet you, thank you. With her hand still in his grasp Nana is led to the living room and seated on the floor until Moseh ssi's mother remarks that a pregnant woman shouldn't be made to sit on the floor, at which point Nana is hurriedly led over to the sofa. Once Moseh ssi and Nana are seated, Moseh ssi's parents claim their spots at either end of it. It's a well-polished plush leather sofa, softly enveloping the buttocks as one sinks gently into it, as though the leather were another layer of skin outside one's own. A short silence follows.

Shall we have some fruit?

Nana stands up to follow Moseh ssi's mother and lend a hand, but her offer to help is flatly refused. Nana sits back down feeling unnerved.

Various knickknacks proliferate in the spacious living room, there's not a lot of empty space. In addition to a large clam-shell planter, an air purifier, a massage chair, and an exercise machine with clothing hanging off of it, there are two glass cabinets displaying fine china and china dolls, and under the drinks table, a stack of bloated, well-thumbed home shopping catalogues. Nana observes these things with care, and breathes in the particular smell that can only be described as the smell of other people's homes.

Moseh ssi had said that he'd lived in this house, with his parents, for twenty-five years. Nana glances at the ceiling, the walls, the front door, reminding herself that Moseh ssi grew up here. She wonders what he was like as an adolescent. Did he slouch about the living room radiating displeasure, face sullen and glowering with discontent? What about when he was a few years older?

With what expression had he come and gone past that wall, with what worries and preoccupations had he walked in and out that door?

Moseh ssi's mother reappears bearing two plates

of pared apple and pear slices. These are small slices, thick layers of the flesh having been removed along with the skin. Nana is perturbed to see how diminished they appear. Each piece of fruit has a toothpick wrapped with red cellophane at one end sticking out of it. Moseh ssi's father grabs a toothpick precisely by its cellophaned end and starts eating. Lips closed, he chomps at the fruit, working his jaw with precision and purpose. Moseh ssi's mother is doing the same, and Nana can see on closer observation that Moseh ssi is too. Nana tries to work her jaw with similar doggedness. They sit and chomp in silence. When the apples are gone Moseh ssi's father grunts, here, and pushes the empty dish towards Moseh ssi's mother. Moseh ssi's mother takes the dish back to the kitchen and returns with more apple slices. The same thing happens with the pears: Moseh ssi's father thrusts the emptied plate towards Moseh ssi's mother, grunting, and Moseh ssi's mother fetches another serving of whittled-down pear.

Silence ensues.

Eventually the silence is interrupted by a few obligatory and intermittent questions: Moseh ssi's mother enquires about Nana's address, age, the baby's due date. Nana's answers are terse. When Moseh ssi's mother asks after her parents, Nana nearly answers

that her father has passed away but that there's Aeja —
then corrects herself and answers that her father has
passed but her mother is still living. Having phrased it
like that, Nana realises that to say her mother is living
is in fact the stranger and more awkward thing to say.
For one thing, it feels odd to call Aeja by something
other than her name, since Aeja is only really Aeja
when you call her Aeja, and then there is the fact that
at present Aeja is possibly closer to merely *being* than
living.

Moseh ssi is generally laconic by temperament,
but at home he seems to have even less to say. All ani-
mation has leaked out of him, he resembles a dummy.
The desultory exchange eventually dries up and neither Moseh ssi's parents nor Nana ventures another
word. Occasionally someone picks up a slice of fruit
and goes back to sitting in silence, but that's the extent
of it. Moseh ssi's mother picks up the remote control, switches the television on. There's an outburst of
laughter: a weekend-night variety show. The four of
them sink deeper into the sofa to watch the screen. A
thought dawns on Nana: this expensive sofa is clearly
positioned to face the television; to these three, all this
amounts to is the usual and therefore entirely familiar
angle, order, and course of their home life.

Work's going well?, Moseh ssi's mother asks with

her eyes on the television.

Yeah, Moseh ssi answers at the television.

It's not too warm at the office?, she asks the TV.

It doesn't matter, Moseh ssi tells the TV, which is an odd way to answer.

Are you working tomorrow is the next question; the answer, it's Monday.

When will the wedding be? Soon.

We haven't really discussed it yet, was the answer Nana had prepared and so I'm more than a little astounded by Moseh ssi's answer. I look over at him, startled, but he keeps his eyes glued to the screen, an inscrutable expression on his face. A moment later he rises from the sofa and announces that he's going for a smoke.

With only three people on the sofa, the soft cushions seem to shift subtly: the balance is broken. Moseh ssi's father, perhaps to correct the imbalance, moves in nearer only to quickly pitch back, as though he's afraid of being too close. Laughter erupts from the television. The earlier awkwardness and unease resurface, along with ennui, causing a restless trepidation in Nana. She's conscious of the stirrings beside her, aware that her slightest movement may prompt an immediate reaction from her neighbours – so she remains tense and unmoving.

They look. Moseh ssi's father and mother look at, but do not see, the television. Instead, it's as if they possess five extra pairs of eyes that are not visible and are, even now, directing nine out of ten my way, and with singularity of purpose. The extra five sets of eyes not angled at the TV roam over, stare at, and examine in turn my wrists, my neck, my feet, Nana's ankles, Nana's toes, Nana's thighs, Nana's belly, chest, ears, hands.

And is there a sexual position the two of you prefer?

Why not ask me that instead? Being quizzed on our sex life would be far more tolerable than this silent scrutiny, Nana is thinking, when a voice asks: And what is it you do? Moseh ssi's mother is looking at the television.

The same thing as Moseh ssi, I am his colleague, Nana answers.

Moseh ssi's mother nods at the television, but it's clear she'd had no idea. How long have you been seeing each other, she asks, nods again when Nana tells her it's been about a year, but now she looks even more puzzled. Eventually she lets out a faint sigh.

That child doesn't say a word when he's home. Never tells you a thing, whatever you might ask. She seems to be addressing herself. She picks up a biro from the stack of catalogues and hands it along with a scrap of paper to Nana, tells her to write down her phone number. She examines the note Nana hands back, folds the paper twice and inserts it between the pages of the topmost catalogue. Moseh ssi's father presses a hand into the sofa seat and resettles himself. Nana rearranges her body so that she's slightly aslant on the sofa. The weekend variety show is over, it's on to commercials.

A lengthy silence accompanies the commercials.

I ask for the bathroom and am told there are two, one here and another there, I am free to use whichever I fancy. I choose the one just off the living room. Flick the light switch on; the fluorescent light above the mirror sputters a couple times and blinks before settling into a dim glow. Step into the rubber bathroom slippers, enter, shut the door behind me. Stand for a moment in front of the mirror marked with dried dots of toothpaste and soap suds; lower myself onto the western-style toilet. Keep my eyes on the floor as I pee, and even when I'm done it doesn't quite feel like I'm done so I sit there a while longer. Flush, take a step towards the washstand – my foot knocks into a roundish brass bowl. The bowl skids heavily over the floor, scraping the tiles. I pause. What is it?

It is a chamber pot. I've only ever seen these on

television, this is the first time I've actually come across one. How fascinating that I was still able to recognise it straight away, I think to myself as I examine it. Its squat, rotund body is almost cute, actually, and pockmarked in places from having been scrubbed clean with metal bristle brushes. The lid has a handle attached to it that resembles the leaf cap of a persimmon. It is an old but well-maintained chamber pot.

—

I need a bath, I think to myself.

As I head home after saying goodbye to Moseh ssi at the foot of the street, I feel a sudden outpour of perspiration. Tepid sweat runs down my armpits, back, and neck. Only then do I realise that I've been sweating the entire day. Where the new sweat runs over the now-dried salty patches, I can feel the skin tingle and itch. I climb the stairs to our flat, my hair and face sodden like I've just had a bucket of water thrown over me. I stand heaving inside the front door, take off my loafers. My body's incomparably clammy; I can't stand it a moment longer.

Let's go for a bath.

At these words, Sora looks up at Nana.

For days now, they hadn't so much as exchanged a single word. Somehow Nana's words have come out sounding angry, but even so she is now in the weaker position of having to wait for Sora's response while the sweat drips from her eyebrows, as though she were at Sora's disposal. Well, even if that were true, there's nothing to be done about it. After all, Nana can't very well scrub her own back in the bathhouse. Which is why it's always been Sora who's scrubbed Nana's back and Nana who's scrubbed Sora's, that's always been the case, there being just the two of us, so you see there's no alternative, there's no other choice. It's just not possible for either of us to sulk for very long.

Is it safe?, Sora asks. Are you allowed to?

So I won't go in the water.

Even so.

Just a quick scrub and we'll be out. Just a quick wash, that's it, and with that I manage to convince Sora, it's decided. As usual, getting a bag of wet items ready – soap, shampoo, and toothbrushes – falls to Sora, and my job is to pack a separate bag of clothes, underwear, and other dry items. We have the routine down pat and are soon headed out the door. We hesitate between Boseok Sauna with its three baths and Hando Sauna which has two, then decide on the latter since we won't be going in the tubs anyway.

Sauna, or bath only?, the woman at the counter asks.

Bath only, we say, and open our wallets to pay the fee. We gather the towels and locker keys she hands us, and head into the changing room. Both the changing room and the bathing area are empty, and we look round at leisure. Perhaps because there's no one but us, it's surprisingly dry and not overly hot. It's just right. Even the floors are mostly dry, and we're able to walk to the row of adjacent taps without getting our feet wet. We choose two seats. It's tempting to sink into the tubs but Nana manages to refrain from doing so; instead she uses the showerhead attached to the tap to wash her body in preparation for the scrub. Nowadays the ingenious invention known as the scrub soap means you can skip the hot tub entirely, since it is as effective at loosening dead skin as a soak in hot water. This is a bonus. Sora and I have always done our own scrubbing – even as children, tough as that was – so to have such a convenient tool at hand is really quite amazing. You lather up the soap and apply it all over your body, then sit on your stool, on which you've already laid down a towel, and wait. This in itself is thoroughly enjoyable. You sit and watch your gleaming pink toes, listening to the sound of your breath in quiet anticipation, and when it feels like the right moment you rinse off the soap and begin rubbing, gently at first. Sora usually begins at her ears, whereas

I start with my wrists. From the wrists, I work my way up gradually, so that by the time I've reached the elbows the grime and dead skin are sufficiently well loosened for a proper scrubbing, and my arm has settled into a proper rhythm. The swish, swish, swish, of the mitt focuses me. Lips pursed, I immerse myself in the task, concentrating all my attention on whichever part of the body I'm scrubbing. Sora is concentrating deeply too, the pair of us going swish-swish, swish-swish, in silence, until at one point I hand my mitt to Sora and turn round so Sora can start on my back. I sit, posture hunched as Sora rubs swish-swish, swish-swish, and then it's my turn to face Sora's back and start rubbing, swish-swish, swish-swish.

Oww that hurts, Sora chides, but swish, swish, I ignore her and keep on, swish, swish, swish. That's enough, swish-swish, swish-swish. The left-hand side of Sora's back is slightly more raised than the right, probably because her spine lists to one side. The bare flesh has reddened with the exfoliation. The sight of her vulnerable exposed back brings up a complex mix of emotions, and I purse my lips even tighter as I continue to scrub.

Swish-swish, swish-swish.

Swish-swish, swish-swish.

The sound fills the large space around us, and I

find this deeply satisfying. Maybe the reason I asked Sora to come bathing with me today was just so I could hear this.

There's a chamber pot at Moseh ssi's house, I blurt out as I work on Sora's back.

A chamber pot, at home.

Whose home?

Moseh ssi – the baby's father.

Father?

He's the father.

And his name is Moseh?

Moseh, Moseh ssi.

And they have a chamber pot at home, I repeat.

It's not as if any of them are ill, really, and their toilet's fully functioning, but still they had one.

Why is that?

I asked Moseh ssi on the way back, and he said his father uses it.

Maybe he's unwell? Maybe he has an illness and needs one?

I asked him that.

And?

He said there was no reason. That he's always used one for no real reason. I asked if his father empties it himself and Moseh ssi said no. His father uses the pot, and his mother empties and cleans it. He said this as if it were nothing. He must have answered as if it were nothing because he actually thinks it's nothing, right? And then he asked me what was strange about it, if it was strange to have a chamber pot, or if I thought chamber pots were weird. Of course they're not. As far as Nana's concerned, you might see one in any number of homes. But what I do find weird, the point of this, is that the father doesn't empty the pot himself but gets someone else to do the job for him. In a house with two perfectly functioning bathrooms, both a few steps away at most – I mean, isn't that weird? To shit or pee in a brass bowl and then leave the cleaning of it to someone else when you live in a house like that?

But it seemed like Moseh ssi had never really considered any of this. He didn't find it at all strange that the person using the chamber pot and the person emptying it would be two different people – and the more Nana thought about it, this seemed to be the strangest part of it. It just doesn't make sense, I can't figure it out: why Moseh ssi is the way he is, why Moseh ssi's father does what he does, why Moseh ssi's mother takes it upon herself to clean the bowl. What kind of dynamic is at work there? What would you say it was? The entire way home I kept going over it in my mind, and still Nana doesn't know. What do you think?

I don't know.

Right.

Maybe that's the point.

What is?

That we don't know, Sora says.

The things we can't seem to figure out no matter how much we think about and how deeply we look into them – maybe these things simply aren't meant to be figured out, they're not meant to be known. Like an unfathomable void. A misuteri, she says, *mystery*, a sort of black hole. And in that family, the black hole happens to be the chamber pot. They may even be aware that the chamber pot is their version of the unknowable. Or maybe they've never even thought about it along these lines – but even so, the point is that some things are impossible to comprehend. That pot may simply be their family misuteri, the black hole in their midst, and it just happens to on their bathroom floor.

Misuteri, Nana hears Sora say, and repeats the word, misuteri, misuteri, until I feel a surge of resentment that makes me pull away from her – thinking this might be it, the reason Sora has come to *not* know, and *not* see: Sora's *mechanism*. I glare at the bare skin on her back, at the strands of wet hair. And in that moment I hear myself say to her small, narrow, wet back – her delicate and therefore hateful back – what are you saying? My voice is trembling.

How can you – what are you *saying*?

Huh?

The bowl – that's why it's there in the first place, because people assume it's not meant to be known. Because no one will think about it seriously, that's why it's there, that's why they go on using it the way they do, can't you see that? Whatever it is, bowl or black hole, the point is to think, to consider it, to give it proper thought.

Proper thought?

Proper thought.

Well, maybe you should take that advice yourself.

What's that supposed to mean?

Why are you keeping it?, Sora asks in lieu of an answer.

Nana stares at Sora's reddened shoulders. Sora turns back to face Nana. Nana's the one who's furious, furious to the point of weeping, but somehow it's Sora's face that crumples as she repeats the question: why did you decide to keep it?

This won't do, Nana tells herself.

Any more talk and Nana might burst into tears, and when Nana cries, Sora cries – which makes Nana cry in turn, and Sora will cry because now Nana's crying, which will make Nana cry which makes Sora cry. This is a given. There won't be any stopping once it's begun, like cogwheels, the mechanism of cogwheels that spin together and against each other on and on and on the moment they're set in motion. Nana knows this and Sora knows it too. This is why Nana hardly ever cries and why Sora hardly ever cries. Hardly ever. To give in to crying is plain unacceptable.

We finish bathing without exchanging another word. Nana's expecting Sora to be cross again and leave without her, but Sora waits in silence while Nana gathers the scattered bottles together. Sora has already soaped the pair of plastic bath stools and basins clean and returned them to their respective spots.

—

We walk home under the summer moon.

It's Nana's second time returning home today, and already close to midnight. She's weary but sleep eludes her. She feels let down by Sora, and she's also grateful Sora didn't stalk off by herself. The human heart is never simple, is it, Nana thinks to herself as she quietly ambles alongside Sora.

Once home, we lay out our wet things on the

veranda and head for the kitchen.

There's an album that belongs to Sora lying open on the kitchen table, with a smattering of small paper flowers, about a dozen or so, scattered next to it. These are flower heads, in fact, having no leaves or stalks, a mix of blooming rainbow pinks and cosmoses.

Aeja made them, Sora says by explanation.

You've been to see her then, Nana asks, to which Sora nods, yes. Sora's cheeks are smooth and clear from the scrub.

It's how she spends her time these days, apparently, folding paper flowers. When I got there, she was busy making them, Sora says and slides a flower across the table.

Nana shifts the pink blossom around on the tabletop. That's nice. It's good to know Aeja's making something. The wind chime hanging by the window tinkles softly. There's a paper blossom stuck to the clapper. Sora must have put it there. But the weight's going to hold down the clapper, there's bound to be less chiming because of it, I think, as I eye the fake bloom.

Since neither of us can sleep, we switch on the television to postpone going to our separate rooms, before eventually fetching the bedding and settling down to sleep right there on the living room floor. Once the lights are off and we're tucked under our blankets, the moon shows itself through the wide-open windows. It's small but luminous, and I follow its slow shift towards the left corner of the window.

What is Moseh ssi like?

Sora's question is unexpected and I pause to consider my answer.

He's not much of a talker.

You should invite him over one day, comes the response, but I hesitate.

Could I, I wonder, invite Moseh ssi here, to this house – are my feelings for him sufficient enough to warrant that?

Do I care that much for him?

Yes. I do care for him. My feelings for Moseh ssi may pale in comparison to Aeja's wholehearted love for Geumju ssi, but Nana does care for Moseh ssi in her own way, and to the degree and density of affection she can muster. He's a man of few words and lacks charm and guile, but he's loveable the more you look at him. Still, it's one thing to find him loveable and quite another to invite him home, Nana's quite determined on this point. To invite him here and introduce him to Sora is to allow the softest, most tender part of Nana's world to come into contact with Moseh ssi. It is to open up the world that no outsider apart from Naghi Oraboni has ever had proximity and access to: the world of Geumju ssi's death and Aeja's almost-death. The part of Nana that appears tranquil but is in fact forever quivering and vacillating – where the most sensitive of her scales are located. More than anything else, Nana's not sure if she wants to open up Sora and Aeja and Nana herself to Moseh ssi, not so much the actual Sora, Aeja, and Nana, but as they exist for her, inside her. Between wishing for things to remain as they are and desiring just as strongly to smash things up, to break everything apart, Nana's internal landscape has been in severe upheaval these days.

Are you asleep, Nana?, Sora asks in the darkness.

The moon has been continuing its trajectory all this while, moving to the right by degrees until it passed out of sight altogether. It's not visible anymore. But its light remains constant. It's a bright glow, luminous enough to cast the ceiling, the walls, Sora's face, all of it in shadow.

—

I'll go ahead and answer that question.

The reason I decided to keep it was because of the dreams, Nana says to Sora.

Dreams?

The recurring dreams.

What sorts of dreams?

These sorts of dreams:

I'm at the grocer's and see a heap of chillies piled high on a stand. A mountain of fresh green chillies. Another day it was clams. I'm looking inside a huge basin that's brimming with water, water so limpid my eyes are refreshed just from looking at it, and I'm thinking, it's so clear, so, so clear as I peer and peer, and that's when I notice a large, clean clam in the water. In another dream, I'm holding something in my hand, and when I open up my palm, I see it's a ring. A silver ring, and as I'm looking at it, a flower blooms out of it, poof – a small red flower blossoming out of nowhere. Then there was the one where I was stuffing peaches into a bag. I kept putting peach after peach into the bag and still it wouldn't fill up, and finally I peek inside wondering what the hell's going on, and that's when I notice the bulge, and I see there's a large white peach already in the bag. Then there was the one about deer. There's a field full of deer. A mob of lush chestnut-brown deer are grazing, and one of them lifts its head and looks straight at me. Its antlers are very pale and grand, and it pads over and thrusts its head at me. The antlers touch my chest. They pierce me. And yet Nana's still standing there, calmly looking down at the deer's neck, think-ing, it's impaled me. In another dream, I was holding one of those gokok, those comma-shaped jade beads, thinking it was an ornamental hairpin. It felt warm to the touch. This hairpin's warm, I thought. Warm and also squishy, it didn't seem fit for fixing one's hair, and I kept worrying at it. These are the sort of taemong I've been having these days and, well, you too, Sora, you had a taemong a while back.

The one with the maple leaf, I add.

True, Sora answers. I did, yes. The maple leaf dream.

Once I heard a song in my sleep, too, I go on. I'm standing under a domed ceiling and listening to the sound of someone singing for a long, long time.

Does that count as a pregnancy dream?

It felt like one.

Felt like it?, Sora asks.

Yeah, I could sense it, that it was meant to be a taemong.

Nana-ya, Sora says after a pause.

Aren't you scared?, she asks. To have a child, to exert all that influence as a parent, then to have to spend the rest of your life watching the child grow into something – to create something that you'll have to constantly worry over, forever – that doesn't scare you?, she asks.

Well, of course I'm scared. Honestly it still hasn't sunk in properly, it still doesn't feel sufficiently real, but yes, it's scary, since there's no knowing how everything will pan out. But maybe it's the not-knowing that makes it frightening. At least that's how I've decided to look at it. I'm determined to bear it, bear with it, despite my fear – I've resolved to do so. To have to resort to resolve, well, that does bring a certain tragic poignancy to it, but nonetheless Nana is resolute. Although in truth this staunch determination is untested, so to start reckoning how it might hold up, well, it's hard enough to know *what* one is supposed to be resolved about, and so along with a certain confidence there's an accompanying sense of vertigo, of one's breath becoming quite faint, but nonetheless Nana's quite adamant, in her own way – all this I want, but fail, to say. Sora must have fallen asleep, or maybe she's deep in thought; in any case she's silent now. I strain my ears, my eyes trained on the ceiling, I listen to the sound of Sora's regular breathing. How could she – how could you ask me that question and fall asleep before I've even answered it, how heartless you are! Heartless, I rant to myself as I pull the blanket up over my chest.

Is it reckless of me?

Nana wonders if she should mention her misgivings to Sora, the moments of uncertainty that grip her.

Is it too irresponsible, to have decided to keep it for that reason?

–

But then I think of the baby, sending me all those dreams in all their different iterations; that's how much this baby wants to be brought into this world.

—

I'll go on.

Being squeamish, I had braced myself for morning sickness, but it turns out I'm not much affected by it. Opening my eyes in the morning, I'll be seized by waves of nausea which won't settle until I've downed a glass of either milk or water, but there hasn't been much vomiting, and in fact my appetite seems to have increased. Morning cravings, Sora calls it. She's heard that some women have cravings instead of morning sickness.

This baby's not too hard on its mum, she says.

With each passing day summer deepens and my body is transformed. The flat belly that made me wonder if there really could be a baby in there has swelled significantly, as have my breasts, and I find my usual underwear too constricting. Any time I've a chance to undress in front of a mirror, I'll lay a hand on the bump or on my back and follow the curve of it. There's a baby in there, I'll tell myself, but the thought remains an abstraction. At most I've confirmed the swells and dips of newly emergent facial features through the shadowy images of the ultrasound, seen the grainy pictures created by reflected sound waves. But the rest of the baby's body may as well be a phantom as far as I'm concerned. It just doesn't feel real. In fact I've got to thinking not that there's a baby growing inside me, but that there's another heart inside. Lying very still on my back at night, I can feel it beating away.

Zig, zig, zig, zig, goes the tiny heart, beating at a faster pace and to a different rhythm than my own. Holding my breath, I have to lie completely still in order to sense the tenuous vibrations. Zig, zig, zig, zig, the fragile and busy motion of this second heart.

That's about the extent of my awareness of the baby, and still my body is quietly and surely under-going a sea change. I'll surprise myself by craving certain things I'd ordinarily never think to eat, or by wolfing down twice the amount I'm ordinarily able to stomach, almost without realising. I hesitate not between whether or not I want to eat a certain thing, but whether or not I can. In all these perceptible and not so perceptible ways, I feel the body transitioning to the maternal body. I'm barely conscious of it, yet it's occurring at a speed I can hardly keep up with, on its own steady headlong course that is by turns wondrous and desolating.

Has there been some progress?

Since the day Nana jotted down her phone number, Moseh ssi's mother has been calling every other day to ask this question in her gravelly voice. She advises, insistently, that Nana settle the matter of engagement and marriage before anyone at work finds out about the pregnancy. But..., Nana thinks to herself. Still she thinks, but.

———

What if you were to go and see Ajumoni?, Naghi Oraboni had said, the moment Nana told him the news.

He was advising Nana to go pay Aeja a visit, together with Moseh ssi. Naghi Oraboni was the first person Nana had told about the pregnancy, and when Nana asked him not to mention it to Sora just yet, he had simply said, I'm sure Sora will treat him well.

As long as he's important to you, that's all that will matter to Sora, and she'll be good to him.

Sora's not that good.

You don't have to be good to treat someone well. It's about her faith in you, Nana. This was the gist of the wrenching conversation that day, already several weeks ago.

As on that day and on all the other days, Nana is sitting across the narrow bar at Wage, watching him as he works. He scores a lattice pattern into a cut of pork and brushes it with soy sauce before throwing the meat onto a gridiron. After a few seconds of watching the fat splatter, he flips the gridiron over. Even more than his cooking, Nana enjoys watching his movements as he cooks: the tidy, streamlined way he weaves about the kitchen stir-frying noodles, whisking eggs, deep-frying vegetables, removing fins, slicing meat. And she likes his hygienic use of the chopping boards.

Naghi Oraboni's hair remains unchanged since childhood, cut in such a way that the locks obscure his forehead. When he's about to start cooking, he gathers all his hair and fixes it in place with a hairband resembling a curved coil spring. Which only brings his face into better focus: the flat, uncreased lids that make his eyes look just like his mother's, the freckles, the familiar reminders of his boyhood face that swiftly and alarmingly transform his features into an old man's whenever he smiles. Or maybe it's the gap in his teeth from a missing upper canine that makes him look old. He showed up with that broken tooth years ago — returning suddenly from a stint overseas — and has never had it fixed. Isn't it high time you got a dental implant or looked into some alternative or other, one might suggest, or taunt him with remarks about how old he looks, but all he'll ever do in response is smile that old-man smile. All he does is smile, infuriatingly.

The three people seated near the entrance get up and leave, and the bar is quiet again. The only remaining patrons are the two women chatting over sautéed beans and beer in the middle of the bar, and Nana who's seated right at the end. Making the most of the lull, Naghi Oraboni grabs a pack of milk from the freezer. He crushes the frozen milk cube, spoons the shaved ice into a glass bowl, adds a sprinkle of roasted grain meal and a drizzle of honey, and then slides the bowl over to Nana. This is an off-the-menu dish that's served exclusively to Nana these days. The other women are intrigued and ask Naghi Oraboni if he serves bingsu as well. They say they'd like to try it too, and plead with him to make them a bowl. Naghi Oraboni smiles uncomfortably at their insistence, but before long he's muttering resignedly, and setting about to prepare a second bowl of shaved ice. The two women fuss over how delicious it is. It doesn't look like much but it's really, really good, they repeat, and start quizzing Naghi Oraboni as they scoop the bingsu into their mouths.

Ajossi, they ask, we've always wondered about this but how old are you, are you married, do you have a girlfriend, what d'you think of her, what about me then? They half-joke half-ask, tittering every time Oraboni makes his politely agreeable one-word replies. Nana scrapes the honey that's dripped to the bottom of the bowl, licks the spoon.

Hmph, she thinks to herself. It's no use, you know. It's no use, your flirting.

And she looks over blankly at Oraboni as he stands there smiling at the women like some gentle soul.

Nana, when she was a child, once had her cheek slapped by Naghi Oraboni.

No, I'd rather not tell this story.

—

I'll go on.

In those days I used to torment small animals for fun.

Puppies, cats, hamsters, the occasional guinea pig. I would step on their tails, poke their paws, squeeze their chests. I didn't find it gratifying or distressing, in fact I felt nothing as I harassed them, and still I persisted in a dazed numbness. We were living in that peculiar split-down-the-middle house at the time, and I was thirteen.

That year Sora had moved on to middle school, leaving me behind in primary school; leaving Nana on her own so that she was alone at lunchtime and alone walking home from school, and since Sora and Naghi Oraboni's schools let out much later than Nana's, she was alone at home too, alone next to Aeja who was immersed in the depths of a desolation all her own, always and entirely, alone.

It was an odd time.

Sora and Nana had been so tightly bound until then, as though they were not two, but one being, and now that Nana was left to herself it felt she was less-than-one. The other half that had adhered to her all this while had dropped away, leaving Nana incomplete, an awkward half. She played alone, marking time by haunting the two deserted spaces at home.

Back then, there used to be a hexagonal fish tank in Naghi Oraboni's living room that was always filled to the top with water. Plastic aquatic plants, thatched houses, and skeletal starfish lay submerged at its bottom, and reddish goldfish swam among the props.

These fish had fat gobstopper bodies and super-fancy fins. If you slid the long glass rod that was used for cleaning the aquarium into the water and swirled it about, the fish would bump into the rod, thud, thud, then swim away, fluttering their fins, terrorised. There was one goldfish that stood out in particular. Amid the red and golden goldfish, this one was a murky black, like a clot of Chinese ink.

It was black and therefore ominous.

I may have told myself that a fish of that colour didn't deserve to be a goldfish. Whatever the reason, I'd spend hours idly chasing after that fish, making it my target. I'd prod its tail fin with the rod and swish, it would change direction and rush off. Follow it as it escaped and poke it again, and swish, off it would dash for dear life. I'd chase the fish like this over and over, relentlessly, chasing and poking, until one day, after chasing the fish into a corner, I happened to press the tip of the rod down on its tail fin. The fish writhed and squirmed to free itself from the rod, rubbing its mouth against the aquarium wall in desperation. In that brief struggle the fin tore and a small piece of it came off. The ripped wisp of fin floated up soundlessly, like ink dissolving in water, then sank back down, then floated up again, and continued to sink and float, over and over, while I watched, transfixed.

At one point I glanced behind me, and found Naghi Oraboni standing there.

I had no idea how long he'd been there, but he looked like a ghost: he was covered in dust, and clumps of earth clung to his hair. Around one eye I could see the beginnings of a bruise, and blood had pooled and hardened into a blackish-red spot on the edge of his lips. Oraboni stood gazing at Nana for a while before heading over to peer at the aquarium. The black goldfish was rapidly closing and opening its mouth as it hovered near the plastic plants. From time to time it would flick its pectoral fins and flip in the opposite direction, as though on high alert. Oraboni observed the fish for a very long time, then straightened his back and turned to face Nana, opened his palm wide, and slapped her across the cheek. He slapped her not once but several times, and as hard as he could.

Does that hurt?, he asked.

Nana looked at him, bewildered.

He repeated the question until she nodded yes.

It doesn't hurt me to do it though, he said sedately, his arm now hanging by his side. I hit you, so you feel pain. It hurts you, but I'm not hurt. I'm looking at you, and I'm not feeling any pain. How does this work then? Since I don't hurt, does that mean you don't either?

He seemed to expect an answer, but Nana couldn't speak, she could only blink at him, a hand cradling her raw cheek.

Oraboni looked straight at her with coal-black eyes. But you do. You hurt, right?

Nana nodded, overwhelmed.

When you were poking the fish, did that hurt you?

Nana shook her head, no.

It's the same, Oraboni said. You and that fish, you're the same.

Does it hurt?, Oraboni asked again.

Seeing Nana nod her head, he told her to remember that, and never to forget it.

Forgetting, that's how people turn monstrous. It's how you become oblivious to other people's pain.

—

Let's visit Aeja this Sunday.

At my suggestion Moseh ssi replied, alright, then asked if I could give that a rest now.

Give what a rest, I asked. Calling your mother Aeja, he answered. He said it made him uncomfortable to hear her being referred to by name.

Does it, I answered, even as I told myself, but Aeja is Aeja. Aeja is more herself when she's called by name, so of course I have to call her Aeja, I thought, half in spite and half, oddly, with disdain.

Sunday arrived, and we set off in Moseh ssi's car with the lunch boxes I'd made with simple home-cooked fare. Moseh ssi's car is silver, a recent model that's shiny and so new even the steering wheel glitters. It's a far cry from Naghi Oraboni's battered old car, you can barely feel the vibrations or hear any hint of the motor. Here I was, being borne off in comfort. My body couldn't have been more relaxed and the weather couldn't have been more ideal, but still a shadow seemed to hang over me. I sensed a dark, severe wrinkle in my mind. Rice balls, rolled omelette, young radish kimchi, spiced aubergine; catching the faint aromas wafting from the lunch boxes, I watched the scenery flow past in silence.

After entering my name in the visitors' book, I sat down in the visiting room with its large circular table and waited for Aeja.

Moseh ssi was serenely looking out the window from his chair.

Outside, the day's heat was at its peak. Not a shred of wind or hint of moisture seemed on hand as the afternoon blazed in the dry-boil of the sun's glare.

At the sound of dragging feet I looked up and saw a girl in her late teens approaching the room. The girl was plump, and her head was bowed, bobbed hair hiding most of her face while her arms held tight a transparent box filled with slippers, sketch books, and stuffed toys, as if it were precious cargo. Mum, she said as she trailed into the visiting room, before halting suddenly, as if disoriented. A nurse followed her in and linked arms with the girl. Mummy's not here. Mummy's at home. Shall we go give Mummy a call. Shall we go and call her together. The nurse continued in a soothing voice as the girl attempted to brush her away with stiff, clumsy movements. Nana was watching this silent stubborn struggle from her spot by Moseh ssi when another nurse appeared and called for Aeja's guardian.

Don't want to move. These were Aeja's words as relayed to them by the nurse, and so it was decided they would visit her in her room. Grabbing the lunch boxes, which were tightly bound in a knotted cloth wrap, they followed the nurse to the level above. Along a corridor that sloped gently upwards, a stair-less incline designed to be wheelchair-accessible, past the nurses' station, a skylight fitted with clear plastic blocks, and a few elderly sunbathing women, and into Aeja's room.

—

Flowers.

Flowers everywhere.

Flowers?

I nod in response to Sora's question before resuming.

The entire room was flowers.

From wall to ceiling, paper flowers dotting out a floral heaven and earth.

Flat and layered, large and small, slender and round and sharp; every single one crafted from paper, hundreds of them lining the wall. There was an overwhelming number of white blooms, with a smattering of red, green, yellow hues, though even these colours lacked in intensity so that the room, on the whole, presented a rather pale, blanched-out prospect. But what flowers were these? What sort of flowers would one say they were? Flowers that would neither wilt nor rot, but merely gather dust as they themselves crumbled to dust. Flower upon flower of the sort.

Nana found them beautiful yet terrible, and she felt herself falter as these emotions churned inside her. Aeja sat in her bed, wordlessly gazing at these people who had set foot in what amounted to the extrusion, the ruptured seepage of her interior life. Nana seated herself on the long bench near the bed and placed the lunch boxes on her lap. Holding down her knees with their weight, she turned to face Aeja. It had been a long while. This person who had been as full of love as her name suggested, until she lost that love – this is, was, Aeja, thought Nana as she looked into the face opposite hers. To this real-life Aeja, who appeared frailer and gentler than the Aeja Nana held inside her, she introduced Moseh ssi. I'm pregnant, and this is the baby's father, Nana explained, while Moseh ssi bowed his head. Aeja seemed unsurprised. She continued to not speak, and merely glanced from Nana to Moseh ssi with her clear eyes.

The lunch boxes were set down and opened, but nobody made a move to start eating. Only after repeated prompting did Moseh ssi give in and take the slice of spiced aubergine that was offered, but no one touched the food after that. The three of them merely sat where they were, staring blankly over the lunch boxes.

On the way down to the parking lot Moseh ssi lit a cigarette and peered down at the lake. In the middle of the lake, the perky lotus buds remained tightly folded, as though waiting to come into flower. Moseh ssi flicked the half-smoked cigarette into the pond. Nana watched as the butt floated, tidy as a piece of chalk, over the black surface through which one could glimpse the snarled tangle of roots.

—

It's past midnight now, making all this part of yesterday's schedule.

I've reached the end of the tale I've been recounting to Sora. We sit facing each other for a while longer, listening to the night shower.

Sora gets up and pads over to the living room window to shut out the rain. Shall we call it a night then, she says. She asks me where I'd like to sleep and I say, here. We bring our blankets and lay them out on the floor. We've increasingly taken to sleeping out here. Tonight, the smell of vinegar and oil from the lunch boxes I made earlier lingers in the air as we prepare our bedding. Once we switch the lights off and lay down side by side, the sound of the rain seems to grow louder. We'd expected a brief shower at most seeing as rain hadn't been forecast, but it's not letting up at all, in fact it's really pouring down now. Perhaps this same rain passed over the care home on its way here. Would Moseh ssi's cigarette have dissolved in the rain? Will it have sunk to the bottom of the lake by now? In the dark, eyes wide open, Nana thinks back to when Moseh ssi flicked his cigarette away. The red glow clinging to its tip: for some reason the moment that glow hit the surface of the lake and fizzled away keeps replaying in Nana's mind.

So, Sora speaks up. So what did Moseh ssi have

to say.

So, Nana repeats silently to herself. That's a secret, she thinks, but does not say.

Let's keep this between us, was what Moseh ssi had said to her. That it would be best to keep it a secret of sorts. But these aren't words Nana could relate to Sora, and so it's a secret. Nana breathes quietly and thinks again. *Of sorts* – how secret is that exactly?

For once, it's cooler outdoors, but we can't open the windows because of the rain, Nana complains in a low voice.

I know, Sora answers.

The rain lets up a bit then starts pouring down again.

It isn't much later that Nana is jolted awake by the sound of the phone ringing. She'd only been asleep for half an hour or so, but her body is leaden, she can barely move. After a struggle Nana manages to raise her upper body, but has to pause again to rest her heavy back, and then, only after a deep sigh, is she finally able to pick up the phone. There's a rustling sound as Sora turns away from Nana.

Hello.

Hello?

—

Listen.

Are you happy, Aeja asks without preamble.

Not waiting for an answer, she asks again, are you happy to be pregnant.

Are you happy. Are you happy. Are you happy.

Are you happy.

Nana listens to the question that's being repeated over and over like a curse.

Why is she asking if I'm happy?

Was Aeja happy, when she gave birth?

Was she happy, after she had Sora and Nana?

Was she, and is that why she thinks Nana would be too, is that why she's asking? Nana feels a chill descend over her, from the top of her head down to her toes, as if she's had icy water upended over her. Her hand feels cold, Nana wonders stupidly if she might not turn into ice right there and then. Sora, who's sitting up now, takes the phone from Nana's freezing hand, puts it to her ear, and listens. Nana hears Aeja's words through Sora's ears.

Listen.

How come the pair of you are happy.

How come you want to be happy all by yourselves.

———

I'll go on.

Sora and Moseh ssi's first encounter came about in a surprisingly simple manner in that Moseh ssi, on his way to pick up Nana, had come to the door, and Sora happened to open the door precisely at that moment. Sora seemed baffled and a bit disoriented, but insisted he come inside and brewed some tea. As Nana recalls, not much in the manner of conversation took place that day. Sora sipped her tea, Moseh ssi sipped his, Nana hers. After that chance meeting Sora would sometimes tell Nana to bring Moseh ssi by again, but for whatever reason Nana didn't feel inclined to do so and kept putting it off as summer progressed. Then the first typhoon of the season was forecast, and with it came news of a death. A sudden tragedy had claimed the life of the cousin who they'd said had gone by the nickname Abdul, his death the result of a traffic accident.

There are two annual rituals Sora and Nana and Naghi Oraboni have observed together over the years.

The first of these is the kimchi-making, the second the making of dumplings with the remainder of the kimchi made the previous year. The former takes place in autumn and the latter in summer.

Naghi Oraboni's mother, Sunja Ajumoni, has a habit of making great quantities of kimchi. If the overripe kimchi is not consumed or otherwise used up by the following autumn, it's impossible to make room for the new batch of kimchi. So every summer, the packed kimchi fridge is emptied of its remaining stock and the overripe kimchi is used to make dumplings. From the simple act of congregating at Ajumoni's place in autumn and marvelling at the sheer quantity of salted baechu cabbage packed into the large basins, the wondering aloud as to whether we we would really make this much kimchi, nagging at her yet again to please reduce the quantity next year as we set about stuffing the salt-wilted cabbages with the kimchi paste, only to be told to leave it alone since making kimchi gives her a sense of gratifying purpose, to the making of dumplings come summer with the last of the previous year's kimchi and finally settling down to eat the fresh mandu – all this constitutes tradition for us. You just have to take all this upon yourself, don't you, we'd grumble, and yet there was no denying that Sora and Nana and possibly even Naghi Oraboni looked forward to these yearly events. So when the season for seeing to last year's kimchi rolled around once more, a date was set for when we would gather at Sunja Ajumoni's.

It was time to make dumplings.

With the weekend just around the corner, we'd gone to shop for the meat. The call from the relative whose name, let alone face, we could barely remember came to Sora. Naghi Oraboni and I were busy choosing the meat, and when I finally turned back I was met by Sora's dazed look. She was still gripping her phone.

He's dead, she said, and I looked at her in bewilderment.

Then you should go, Oraboni said. You should go pay your respects.

As it happened the relative had apparently advised Sora that we attend, saying the pair of us were now old enough to do what was right and start showing up to these things. Hearing this Nana was incensed. What freaking duty, she thought. This from the same people who had behaved with such crude indecency over Geumju ssi's wrongful death settlement and over Aeja, and now they had the nerve to say this.

Let's not go.

What would be the point, Nana argued, but Sora said, still, and Oraboni quietly, insistently, sided with Sora until it was finally decided that we would attend the wake. We headed back home to change into something black. Nana stubbornly and with some malice insisted that Naghi should come too, so that finally all three of us set off for the funeral hall.

What would we do there anyway, Nana asked, but

what she meant was, what are we supposed to say to them?

What would we say?

It wasn't that there weren't things to say. No, in fact, there was too much that needed saying and one scarcely knew where to begin. And the funeral hall would be teeming with relatives. Nana's mind churned less from knowing the cousin was dead or from any grief over his death, but out of sheer apprehension at having to confront the relatives – especially in that place. So much to say. Much too much of it. I want to say it all. Standing right in front of them, looking them squarely in the face, I want to ask them, want to hear them answer, I want to finally say it, get it off my chest. All of it. All of it, entirely.

How lonely Sora and Nana have been; how much they have, in all this time, and silently, resented them all. Nana got herself worked up just thinking about all this, and death couldn't have been further from her mind with all the inner rage that gripped her through the drive out there in Oraboni's ancient car.

It's not my place after all, the two of you should go on in without me, said Naghi Oraboni, so Sora and Nana left him in the parking lot and walked together to the funeral hall. As expected, the place was swarming. Even Grandmother, whom Nana at their last encounter had imagined seeing at the altar of a funeral hall, as a funeral portrait, was present amid a nest of relatives, clad in funereal black and glaring at the condolence-paying guests. And there now was the cousin's face, peeping out from the portrait that was nearly smothered in rows of white and yellow chrysanthemums. Taking turns with Sora, Nana made an offering of incense, then stood and clasped her hands respectfully in front of the portrait before raising her eyes to gaze into the young face.

She had only one memory to remember him by, from the day they'd gone to eat duck meat.

Nana had agreed to go along that day purely out of a mostly hostile curiosity, and she had scarcely paid attention to the cousin. A single thought had preoccupied her: how she would demand of Baekbu and Baekmo, who in all these years had not once bothered to ask after Aeja, why they had not done so. And though in the end she couldn't bring herself to go through with it, this interrogation had been the only thing on her mind that day.

Zig, zig, zig, zig.

There must have been a time when this cousin's heart, too, beat as quietly and as busily.

As there must have been a day when her aunt, in stillness, first felt it beating inside her.

The once spirited and proud Baekmo sits slumped on the floor, surrounded by people in mourning clothes. Her hands bound in the grip of a priest who is offering up a prayer, her profile clenched in anguish as if her eyes and lips are never to be reopened. Now that Nana's set foot in the hall, her earlier resolve seems to have vanished, she feels cowed and nervous as she eyes her aunt. When the prayer ends Baekmo collapses onto the floor, prostrating herself before the cross-legged priest.

There's no use... how can I believe in any of it now... I can't believe in God... I can't, not now... Father, what am I to do now, what about my son, what about my baby..., Nana hears the sporadic trail of words. Everybody is listening with bated breath.

By now Baekmo is lost from view in the press of people about her – she's reduced to her voice. There's not a sound to be heard otherwise, no low rumble of conversation or even the clattering of chopsticks, nothing but this submerged voice, its foundering blood and temperature almost palpable.

To lose one's child.

Nana has never known such crushing agony.

Mid-inhale her breath caught, as involuntary a spasm as a hiccup.

And finally it dawned on Nana.

It dawned on her that having been so intent on her own pain, it hadn't occurred to her to consider the unequivocal anguish now presented before her. And that this made hers the closest likeness to that heart which Nana wholly detested, namely, Aeja's heart. That she had been entirely oblivious of the lesson that Naghi Oraboni had so memorably impressed upon her by slapping her across the face all those years ago.

That's how people turn monstrous.

Don't ever forget it.

That she had at every moment erased from consciousness, almost as a matter of course, this excruciating plea.

—

Below the raised entrance of their section of the funeral hall, there were so many shoes scattered about it was difficult to tell which one paired up with which. Standing at the end of the maru, Sora and Nana had to scan the crammed space – there was literally no room to put a foot in edgewise – before finally spotting their own. Properly shod, they returned to the parking lot. Oraboni was waiting by the car, getting some air. He's perched at the edge of a flowerbed with its small red pine and purple bloom maples, his hands tucked in his trouser pockets. As their eyes meet, he lifts his chin in the afternoon shade as if to say, hey. He's squinting in the light. He looks old, even though he's not smiling. Astonishingly so.

This man whose childhood Nana knows intimately.

You know what.

I wanted to make a baby with you.

That there was a time when Nana had held such a wish, is a secret.

—

I'll go on.

After that initial meeting, it appeared that Sora and Moseh ssi came to be on nodding terms with each other: Sora would happen to see Moseh ssi waiting downstairs for Nana just as he happened to peer up at the window, and they would bow their heads in greeting.

One day, Sora said to Nana after gazing out the window, he never says hello, does he.

Never says hello?

Now that I think about it, Nana tells herself. Yes, she doesn't recall hearing him say hello. When has she heard him utter the word to anyone. Surely it can't be never, surely it must just be a rarity, but no matter how she ransacks her memory, she comes up with nothing. Not once. Not ever. She may have seen him nod his head in greeting now and then, but saying hello to someone is something she has neither seen nor heard him do.

Has there been some progress?

Moseh ssi's mother continues to ring round every other day with this question. In January, they say the seventh is auspicious.

Auspicious?

For the baby, she answers.

With the phone pressed to my ear I raise my head. I can see Moseh ssi over the office partitions. He's looking at something, head buried in his desk. Moseh ssi's mother continues, the baby's due in January, and since the seventh is the best day that month that's when the baby should be born. I see, I answer. Well, it would be nice if that's the day, if it's said to be the best day for it. But it's not down to me after all, I can't will the baby into coming. At this Moseh ssi's mother shoots back, but you must.

That's the best day so we'll have to open you up then.

I'm sorry?

We have to open you up.

Open me up?

Operate, to match the date.

Everyone does it these days, she says firmly. I try to digest what it is she's just said to me. I feel a chill through my body. I am horrified. Truth be told, nothing Aeja has ever said has come close to frightening me to this extent.

But won't that be painful?

This is met by a snort that's verging on ridicule.

There's no getting around it anyway, is there?

—

Recently, I keep thinking back to my first date with Moseh ssi, when we'd gone for a drive out of the city to the arboretum.

We had settled into a quiet routine where we'd each do our work at the office then go for dinner together, after which Moseh ssi would walk me home and we'd say our 'see you tomorrow's, and the next day, just as we'd said, we would see each other at work. One time we were having lunch on our own near the office, and noticing how clear the skies were, I happened to say, more to myself than out loud, how I'd like to go somewhere further afield. Moseh ssi asked where I'd like to go. Just a bit afield, I answered ambiguously, and then forgot this little exchange, but Moseh ssi came back to me with the same question a few days later. At first I replied that there wasn't anywhere particular I had in mind, really, but he was persistent and repeated the question several times, until finally I answered, without giving it much thought, an arboretum. An arboretum, he said, nodding his head, seeming to make a mental note of it. Then, the following weekend, he just showed up at Nana's doorstep with a large picnic hamper in hand. In the car, Moseh ssi drove carefully while telling Nana the story of the arboretum they were about to visit. They say it's a primeval forest. And that there's a conjoined tree that grew together out of the scars of war. From the passenger seat I listened and nodded my head, but in fact I was thinking how typical of humans to drape even the trees of an ancient forest with significance, trees that were perfectly fine growing and intertwining as was their wont, and then to act all solemn. How incorrigible, I thought drearily as I was driven on.

After a two-hour drive, we arrived at the arboretum to discover it was closed to visitors that day. We had come during the conservation period when they temporarily closed off the woodlands as a protective measure against the flood of visitors. Heavy, striped barricades of black and yellow prevented access to the sloped path that led up to the woods. Moseh ssi stood and gaped at the forest beyond, seemingly rooted to the spot. Holding on to the hamper – an actual picnic hamper filled with sandwiches and grapefruit and carbonated water and metal knives and forks and even ceramic plates – he muttered, what now, in a low voice, his round ears flushed pink, a lost look on his face. The knuckles of his hand were blanched from the weight of the hamper. Nana felt a surge of compassion.

I'd only mentioned the arboretum for the sake of answering.

Moseh ssi was a clumsy, awkward person who'd gone to all this trouble, and all because of a random remark.

How lovely, Nana had thought.

—

He's lovely, and loveable – but this won't do.

When did this thought first begin to take shape?

I'll tell you.

There's no getting around it anyway, is there.

Following that curiously cold and, depending on how you heard it, belittling tone that ended the phone call, I finally confronted Moseh ssi with the question that had been eating away at me for some time. I did so at a salad bar, where we'd stopped to grab dinner on our way home one evening. Perhaps it wasn't the proper place for such a conversation. I'd been staring into my plate, focusing on the greens I'd forked out of the carved rubberwood bowl, and then I said, about the chamber pot...

Moseh ssi lifted his head as if to ask, chamber pot?

Yes, the chamber pot. Has your mother ever mentioned what she thinks of it, whether she likes or dislikes it, I asked.

Moseh ssi worked his jaw for a good while, unaware of the speck of egg yolk clinging to his lips. She hasn't.

No?

That's right. She hasn't, Moseh ssi repeated.

Have you never wondered about it? Wondered why your father gets other people to empty it, why your mother empties someone else's chamber pot, have you never wanted to ask these questions and see what they might have to say—

But this was as far as she got as Moseh ssi cut her off, saying, what do you mean, other people?

They're not other people.

Aren't they?

How are they 'other people'?

But they are.

They're family.

And that means they're not other people?

Of course it does, Moseh ssi said firmly, then speared a carrot with his fork, dislodged it, started chewing. In that moment Nana found him so singularly unfamiliar, she could only gape at the sight of him. Not other people? Is he being earnest right now, she wondered. Does he think his parents know everything there is to know about one another then, because they're not other people. Or that there's no need to know more or even be curious because they're known quantities to one another? Whereas Nana's forever discovering things she doesn't know, whether about Aeja or Sora or Naghi Oraboni or Moseh ssi right this instant, so many things she's unaware of. All these *mysteries*, even among family.

What about you, then? You're part of the family too, so have you ever emptied the pot?

Why do you keep asking about this?

Because I'm curious.

Moseh ssi exhaled loudly, slumped back in his seat, then said, they're married, aren't they? They're husband and wife, aren't these things a natural part of married life? Then, as if to declare the matter closed, he lunged forward and resumed ploughing through the salad. Nana looked at the olives on her plate, nudging them with her fork. She thought, so that's what being husband and wife means to him. That's what family means to him: no longer counting as other people. Then will Nana, too, once she becomes part of his family, cease to be someone other? That peculiar manner his family has of watching TV – or is it a form of conversation more than a form of watching TV maybe – and will Nana start addressing the TV too, one day? Directing all her questions and answers at the television even though the person's seated right next to her – yet still counting as family and not other people. Is that what it means to be a regular family? Could it be that Nana and Sora simply don't know, never having experienced such a thing. And yet…

And yet, Nana reminds herself.

He was the one who wanted to keep the Aeja business a secret.

That it would be best not to tell his parents about Aeja being in a care home, it had been his idea. But why was that? It's fine to have family who don't count as other people deal with your excrement, but Aeja must be kept a secret – why? Why must Nana keep her a secret? Why is that best? Why won't Moseh ssi think about these things as he should, properly? With her empty hand Nana picked up the knife that lay on the table, but she found its cold, metallic weight disturbing and put it back, resting both her hands on her lap. Moseh ssi, she called to him, as he sat wordlessly attending to his salad with a sullen expression.

You're sure – you're set on marrying me?

Yes.

Because of the baby?

And since it's the order of things.

The order of things?

It's the natural thing to do, isn't it?, he asked in reply, to which Nana answered, no, it isn't.

I have no wish to marry you, Moseh ssi.

—

It's been a long wait, I know.

After the various delays, dumpling day is finally here.

For Sora and Nana and Naghi Oraboni, home-made mandu are called Sun mandu, after the Sun in Naghi's mother's name. There's no special recipe or method, apart from the generous amounts of meat, tofu, and kimchi involved, the generosity being entirely determined by Sunja's hand measurements. And of course, the mandu skins are made using dough prepared by Oraboni. That's all, and yet this last is a crucial element, when the dough is mixed or worked by someone else it never gives the precise taste and texture that makes Sun mandu. Before getting down to the actual mandu-making, Oraboni first prepares the dough, kneading it in the bowl he grips in place with his thighs. He works at it until the surface is smooth and springy, covers the dough in cling film and leaves it to rest in the bowl for several hours at least, and when the wrap is finally removed, the fermented dough will have risen to a soft, luke-warm ball. One then breaks a piece that's roughly the thickness of one's thumb, which looks good enough to put straight in the steamer and eat as it is, and sets to work. The piece of torn-off dough is placed on a floured chopping board then rolled out to just the right thickness – mandu skin should be neither too thin nor too thick. The mandu are shaped into two groups: flat for frying, and pursed and round for steaming or boiling. This is the basic rule, but it's not set in stone, of course, so from time to time we will try out fat leaf shapes, or slender half-moon shapes resembling songpyun.

This year, it seems there's more than the usual amount of ripe kimchi to use up, meaning we'll have a daunting number of dumplings to turn out. Maybe we could invite Moseh ssi over, Sora proposes, but Nana answers, best not. Did you argue? Sora asks. He's angry, Nana replies.

I can't marry you, Moseh ssi.

I don't want to be a family, not with you.

Since the day Nana uttered these words, Moseh ssi has been quietly and wordlessly raging.

What does that make us then? Not married, not a family — what are we then, he'd asked in response, and in the ten days since hasn't spoken to her, hasn't come near her. At the office they go about their separate business, lunch apart, and only at the end of the day does he glance over at Nana after tidying his desk. As if he's waiting for Nana to come to him and apologise, to say let's forget what I said before and walk home together. Nana looks regretfully over the partition at him, but she can't cede ground, not on this, she does not head over to him. Guilt gnaws at her, she feels she's abandoned him, and still she cannot approach him.

Listen.

As they're picking out a watermelon to bring to Sunja Ajumoni's, Nana confesses that she has decided to raise the child alone. It won't do with Moseh ssi. I've decided it won't do. The words tumble out bluntly, and Nana's heart blunts in turn. Sora nods as if to say she understands, looking down at the plums. Watching Sora's tame reaction, the sudden tensing she can sense in Sora, it occurs to Nana that she may be the bully, that, in fact, Nana maybe the worse of the two after all. What does Sora think? What are you thinking right now? You resent Nana, don't you? Aren't you blaming Nana even now? Why don't you ask anything more about it? Why won't you ask what needs asking, properly? These questions race through Nana's head but she's unable to voice any of them which means perhaps that it is in fact Nana who is the delicate one. How sly, to be delicate. Nana bows her head, dizzy with the swarm of thoughts, when Sora reaches out and briefly grabs Nana's ring finger, lightly holding it with her hand.

The baby's fine. It's got its auntie, it's fine.

You hate it, though. I know you think of babies as a nuisance.

You're right, I do.

See.

But liking anything straight off the bat, no questions asked, isn't that also suspicious in its way? So what I'm saying is – try and depend on me, she adds in a thin voice. But Nana thinks there's no way she can believe those words. She can't trust the words of someone who's frailer than Nana, physically and otherwise, Nana tells herself as she swallows back the warm prickling sensation rising up at the back of her throat.

—

Aunt Sunja lives on the upper floor of a two-storey detached house. Nana tramps up the exterior staircase. Being roofless and exposed to weather, these long, steep stairs, with their sluicing rain in summer and drifts of snow in winter have been carefully maintained by Naghi Oraboni over the years. Nana has never let on that she knows, but she knows that he makes sure to stop by on snowy days. At the first sign of snow he will come by with a bag of coarse salt. First he'll use the broom hanging at the top of the stairs to sweep the snow off each step; once he has reached the bottom step he clears the snow from the foot of the stairs all the way to the front of the house in a large fan shape; finally he climbs back up the steps, scattering salt as he goes. Nana saw him do this herself, very early in the morning one day. She'd dropped by the house for dinner the evening before then stayed the night, finding it bothersome to go home afterwards. Early in the morning she'd heard the sound of sweeping, and when she looked out, there he was. Somehow she'd felt she couldn't let him know he'd been seen, and had watched from the room instead. Until he hung the broom back in its place, thumped his wet gloves together before tucking them away in his jacket pocket, descended the steps and headed down the street.

—

We're here, we call out as we step past the front door.

The door is ajar, a double layer of faux bamboo shades hang from the frame. Oraboni has come early to prepare the dough. He greets us now at the door and takes the watermelon sling off our hands. You needn't have, Ajumoni says, but she seems happy to see the fruit. She gets the chopping board straight down, halves the watermelon, covers the two halves with cling film and stores them in the fridge. All the while she's asking after Nana, how's the belly, she asks, then tells Oraboni to get the new floor cushions out. The living room is already in disarray with all the paraphernalia needed for today's dumpling-making, and in the middle of this Sora is served a glass of sweet rice drink, Nana a glass of barley tea. Nana is thirsty; she downs the cold tea at once and heads to the kitchen with her glass begging to be allowed some of the rice drink, too, but she's told it's not a suitable drink for pregnant or breastfeeding women. Why, Nana asks; because it dries up the milk, comes the reply, then, sharper but in a sunny voice, you drink what I give you, missy. There's a scent of apples in sawdust. It's years now since Ajumoni stopped selling fruit, but in her house and on her body you can still smell it, the scent of crated fruit. Nana looks at the ruddy face, now permanently sporting a brownish cast from the years of repeated freezing and thawing in open air. It's been four months since she was last here. They always feel short, the gaps in between, until one thinks back and realises it's been months, a fact Nana finds both poignant and frightening.

Ajumoni or Omoni; aunt or mother.

Both terms are used, according to whatever feels natural in the moment, but unlike Aeja it is impossible to address her as Sunja. For one thing, Oraboni doesn't call her by name.

Sunja and Aeja.

Nana finds herself dwelling on this from time to time.

That having been raised on the food prepared by Ajumoni, a home meal, as far as the sisters are concerned, can only rightly mean the rice and banchan of this particular home. Ajumoni's cooking, the food made by her hands. Steeped as they have been in the flavour of her home cooking since childhood, no matter what delectable and fine food they may come across now, anything that's not of this home is simply – for Sora and Nana both – other, the taste of not-home.

And yet Nana also finds herself pondering a different question from time to time.

She wonders if perhaps the full force of Aeja's heart and devotion isn't more complete, in fact, than that of Sunja's heart and devotion.

Occasionally she'll think this, without letting on, which perhaps makes Nana most like Aeja in temperament after all.

And this is precisely the reason Nana is wary of such wholehearted devotion in the first place.

—

One is bound to ruin one's clothes while making dumplings, so work clothes are essential. Nana changes into the work pants Ajumoni has handed her in the room with the dressing table that's laden not so much with cosmetic products, but with various knickknacks that have been put aside temporarily as one comes and goes – and just like that, her bearing immediately resembles that of Sunja Ajumoni. She settles down comfortably on the floor, facing the large stainless basin of filling mix, and realises that her pose, too, is identical to Ajumoni's. She'd missed this, she tells herself. What had been lacking, decisively so, in Nana's life of late could very well have been precisely this, she thinks.

Eat mandu for the filling, eat songpyun for the skin.

So Ajumoni declares as she pours in the final ingredient for the filling, long green onions, into the basin. These come last. Added too early, their hollow leaves will only become crushed and ooze out slime, making everything stick and smell. Nana learned this from Ajumoni. Now she deftly mixes in the onions with a few light movements, as she's been taught to do. Next she picks up a piece of mandu skin that Oraboni and Sora are rolling out, lays it on the palm of her hand, fills it, then folds the ends together to seal it. As the two steps progress at different speeds, once there's a pile of mandu skins Oraboni or Sora will switch to the filling, and switch back again when they start to run low. Once sealed, the dumplings must be pressed gently in flour before being laid out on the trays to prevent sticking. Arranged in neat rows, the dumplings made by Sora and Nana and Oraboni are all of a different shape. Ajumoni gathers these by the trayful and steams them over the boiling pot. That this initial steaming is a necessary first step in preventing the dumplings, even the ones that are to be stored in the freezer, from bursting later on is another lesson passed on from Ajumoni. We go on slowly rolling and folding in the ways we have been taught, wiping the beads of sweat off our brows in the steamed-up space, and taking little breaks by turns to eat slices of peaches and watermelon as the dumplings take shape at one end and emerge from the steamer on the other. The big table mainly used for jesa is soon entirely covered, as are various other surfaces in the living room, with tray upon tray of the increasingly translucent, cooling mandu – dumplings that are both collectively, and independently, ours.

A plate of steamed dumplings is brought out so we can gauge the newly mixed filling for saltiness; Nana grabs one with her floured hand, pops it in her mouth.

How is it?

Delicious, she answers.

It's really good.

Really, really good.

The longing, the delight, the tenderness, the fear, the loneliness, the regret, the joy – all muddled, all at once.

All one big mess.

—

To wrap up dumpling day, we share bowls of mandu soup.

That is the unspoken rule.

But today, just as we were about to drop the dumplings in the steaming, boiling water, we realised we were out of eggs. Ajumoni likes to stir in some eggs right at the end to add a bit of cheer, she says this makes the soup less lonesome, and Sora and I have come to agree with her over the years. Oraboni had already volunteered to go, but I stopped him, saying I'd like to get some air and stretch my legs. It was nearly sundown. After picking up some eggs and biscuits from a corner shop, along with a carton of milk, I was walking back home, the plastic bag dangling in my hand, when I spotted Moseh ssi. He was standing with his back to the closed shopfront of the soy milk supplier's, staring up the stairs to Ajumoni's front door. I had flour on my front, flour on the hems of the pants, even my hair was streaked with dried dough; the thought of my appearance made me feel depleted, all of a sudden, and somewhat embarrassed.

Moseh ssi, I called out, and he turned towards me with a gloomy face, melancholy hovering on the edges of his clamped lips. How did you know to come here?

I followed you.

From where?

Moseh ssi hangs his head and says, from your place. I was waiting for you, then I saw you leave, so.

You've been out here all this time?

Yes.

Why, I stopped myself from asking, and merely

looked at him.

Nana ssi, do you dislike me? Have your feelings changed, Moseh ssi asked.

No.

Then let's live together.

I don't want to.

We have to be a family, Moseh ssi answered.

Moseh ssi.

I do care for you.

But I can't be the kind of family you want.

You're selfish, Nana ssi. You're only thinking of yourself. What about the child? What about the social *dehmiji* to the child as it grows up?

Damage? What an odd moment to use an English term! It's quite adorable, actually, I was thinking, when I was gripped by the shoulders. Moseh ssi's face loomed close, I noticed how gaunt and fatigued he appeared in just a few days. His thumbs stabbed my shoulder blades, he seemed intent on piercing the skin, but I was too overwhelmed by the force of his eyes staring into mine to really register the pain. What about us, Moseh ssi said.

Are you determined to raise a child without a father. When I'm here? When it has a father? When it's my child? Don't I have a right to the child too? What about me then. And what about us? What are we then? What are we to be to each other? To have a child together but not marry each other? What do we do, take turns raising the child? Is that the sort of thing you want? How is that a family? How does that make sense? Does that make sense to you? Does it. Does it, I say.

Clutched narrowly by both shoulders, his hands thrust in her neck, Nana's whole body being shaken to and fro.

It was excruciating.

Perhaps he'd only grabbed Nana out of sheer desperation, but his thumbs were digging into her throat now, were in fact throttling her with their unyielding strength, and still he remained oblivious, still he wouldn't relent. Instead his hands tightened further around Nana's neck with every word he was willing her to hear.

This won't do.

I might lose consciousness if this goes on.

And with that thought Nana reached out to grab Moseh ssi's arm. As her nails tried to find purchase on his clammy forearm, Moseh ssi knitted his brows together, but didn't relax his hold around her neck. His lips continued to spew words, but Nana was no longer able to make out his words, she was choking, she heard nothing. Silently and wordlessly, she was being strangled.

Zig, zig, zig, zig.

A sudden dull pounding, near the tail end of the backbone. Shocked, Nana swung her arms about, sensed nail clawing skin. Distantly registered the drops of blood springing up on Moseh ssi's left cheek. Moseh ssi, Nana thought, her neck still in his choke-hold.

Doesn't it hurt?

—

Don't ever forget it.

Anytime you hurt, remember that other people can hurt just as much. You've got to make that con-nection. But most of the time, that connection, it might not happen as often as we'd think. Most of the time it might seem more natural to pretend other-wise. But that's why we've got to remember. Because if we don't, we'll forget, entirely.

And forgetting, that's how people turn monstrous.

—

Dusk; the light of the setting sun was dazzling. Even behind closed lids, my eyes were basked in vivid orange.

My feet lifted off the ground, and in the same

instant, I heard shouts. A staggering blow, Moseh ssi's hands falling away in the impact, and with that Nana buckled to the ground, her legs gave way. Free of his grip at last, her throat still felt constricted, and she found it difficult to breathe. She was crouching on the ground, hacking and wheezing, when she heard Sora's voice. Sora's voice shouting, Nana-ya, you, how dare you, you dare, to Nana, you're not getting away, I'll show you, I'll not, you won't, yelling out a jumble of words like a deranged ghost. What are you saying, Nana thought. What do you even mean.

You're not making any sense.

Can't you speak properly, and with that, a wail erupted from my lips.

It still makes me furious.

Because I'd unwittingly cried out, Unni-ya.

I'll go on.

NAGHI

鏍其

Do you believe in past lives?

I don't.

Once, in a previous life, I was killed in a blast.

So I believe, without believing in past lives.

There's a recurring dream I have.

I don't dream it so much as jerk awake from it, jolted into consciousness by the thunderous blast. Boom, and a single sliver of me soars, falls splat on the ground. The left cheek, I'd say. And I must have been born into this life still holding on to that sliver of memory, because I can't seem to shake the moment from my mind and am constantly reliving it. This I do believe.

I am persistent; I cling to the trace of the past life in this one.

I am nothing if not dogged.

Dogged in my waiting for you.

The left cheek, I'd say.

Or rather left face may be more accurate. The left-half of the face, a cloven mask of lone ear, lone eyelid, and lone eyebrow. As it rose up, the half-face appeared almost to be in a trance, near ecstatic, horribly gashed, yes, but the single closed eyelid granting a still serenity to it. But perhaps what I witnessed was someone else's final moment and not my own.

Perhaps it was your death I witnessed.

In which case I am the rememberer not of my own past life but of yours.

A person who has witnessed a death that was yours.

It may be your death, then, that I await with such dogged persistence well into this present life.

Lately I have been mulling over this possibility.

It has been too long since I last saw you.

—

On nights like this when my eyes jar open, an image rises to the surface.

A hut enveloped in snow.

A perpetually snow-swept landscape, no matter the actual time of year.

—

My mother lived through the war as a child.

After losing everyone in her immediate family as they fled to safety, she was left to straggle behind some relatives in search of refuge until the war ended, then wound up under the care of a grandfather living upcountry. By then she was seven years old. Her grandfather's hut sat in a small basin hemmed in by mountains that were remote and unpeopled, and this was where she lived for the next three or four years. It was a substantial period of time, sufficient for her to have gathered a handful of memories of the place, but for some reason I only seem to recollect the winters, she used to say to me. Her grandfather was a man of few words. All through the winter, days would go by without a single word being spoken, sometimes a fortnight. Mornings and evenings, she would open the door of her room onto the snowy landscape, and her ears were always blocked, likely from the temperature and the altitude, she said. Her grandfather would rise at dawn, kindle firewood for the rice; later he'd scrape the crispy, slightly burned rice from the bottom of the heavy cast-iron gamasot, and leave a bowlful by the floor where she slept, near her pillow. The first thing she saw when she opened her eyes and rolled onto her belly was the wheat-coloured nurungji. Everyday there it would be, by her pillow, and that made her glad, she used to tell me. It was the one cheery thing in that perpetually blanched landscape where the snow seemed to cloak the entirety of human emotions, and this made her glad.

Then one year when spring arrived, an aunt made her way inland to fetch Mother. She was brought to the city, to live near market. The aunt promised to send Mother to school and marry her off to a good man once she'd settled in, but in fact Mother barely had a spare moment to herself, let alone to read or study, for she became her aunt's maid, and her days were filled with housework and the care of an infant baby. Once the baby was old enough she was made to help out at the market shop selling hot soup with rice. Mother's aunt refused to hire anyone to save on expenses; instead she worked Mother for the price of three meals, a place to stay, and a small allowance, and it was only after Mother had reached her mid-twenties that she finally married Mother off to a man they knew from the market, with a new set of blankets as a dowry for the honeymoon home. The popular saying about how family means you make concessions for the other must have served my mother's aunt very well. To this day Mother keeps in touch with this aunt, and their relationship is neither good nor bad. After all, if it hadn't been for her I might have lived my whole life in that valley with Grandfather and never known any other life, is how Mother put it to me once.

But there was this one day, she'll say from time to time, launching into a familiar story.

One day Grandfather turned up at the market.

A year or two since Mother's aunt had come to fetch her away from the valley, he'd simply appeared at the shop, bundled up in heavy winter clothes like an elderly peasant. My mother's aunt decided he had come to steal her niece away and said she wanted nothing to do with him, she wouldn't offer him a bowl of soup, or even acknowledge him. Why he'd ventured to the market when he avoided crowds on principle was a mystery, but in any case my mother seems to have deeply regretted this incident, and every now and then she'll describe again the slight, wispy old man, how he'd sat disregarded at the edge of the shop floor, before finally getting up to make his way back, on an empty stomach, to that remote hut.

He lived out the rest of his days alone in that hut, and died there, alone. His grave lies near the Military Demarcation Line. It's an area that's mostly off-limits to civilians; if you wish to visit the grave you must first obtain permission to enter, and you must be accompanied by an armed soldier. Once there, you'll find the grave on a steep slope, looking out to the

north as if it were awaiting something. Every autumn
Mother packs up some dried fish, some fruit, and
liquor, and makes her way to the grave. The area is
mostly untouched by human feet, the scurrying paws
of small animals making up its main traffic; any trace
of our bushwhacking the previous year will have vanished under overgrown grass and foliage, forcing us to
reorient ourselves and beat a new track up the slope
in the right direction. Carrying a small bundle of food
for the jesa, Mother will make her way up the dim,
slippery slope where sunlight never seems to reach.
When we've finally reached the grave she'll call out,
it's Sunja, Grandfather, I've come. As she sets to work
smoothing over the dents and gouges left by wild
boars grinding their tusks and digging their hooves
into the grassy knoll of the tumulus, she complains
every year that she's a granny herself now, she can't
be trekking up here again next year, she hasn't got the
energy for it. But we did visit last year, and since she
hasn't said otherwise, we're sure to be going this year
too. These last couple of years Mother's health has
been troubling her, and I tried to dissuade her from
going, but she replied that as long as she's living she'd
like to visit no matter what, seeing as no one else will
be tending his grave once she's passed on.

By now, I imagine there must remain only the

faintest traces of the hut ever having been there.

I've never seen the hut myself.

Mother would hold a summary jesa, laying out the apples and pears and dried pollack strips at the grave, and throwing liquor over the grass. When that was over she'd pass a glass to the soldier who'd accompanied us there, saying it would warm him up some. Some refused, saying they were on duty, but mostly they accepted, and would sit off to one side and peer down the hill as they ate and drank what we'd shared. Mother and I would sit with our backs to the grave and look out at the mountains opposite.

The mountains were invariably autumnal. The parched leaves would rattle from the branches in the wind, and there'd be a nip in the air. Mother would sit and gaze out beyond the rippling ridgelines before saying, somewhere over there, that's where the house should be.

I find myself thinking about that hut sometimes, almost as if I have seen it when in fact I've never laid eyes on it.

It's a snowy landscape, exactly as my mother described.

At the bottom of the basin there is a tiny house.

Any trace of all who've entered and departed from it over the years has been smothered in snow. The basin is entirely blanketed and indistinguishable from the overcast sky, just as the dimly rising ridgelines behind the house are indistinguishable from both sky and basin. The hut seems to have erupted out of white silk. This is the hut where my mother's grandfather, my great-grandfather once lived. Every time I picture his house, I like to imagine that he still lives there, he whose face I've never seen. That day and night he keeps a light on in that dark hut of his.

For he is waiting. Or so I imagine.

Occasionally, when there's a lull, when the patrons have left and the bar is quiet, or as I'm peering into the bin full of onion skin I've been peeling from my stool, or as I'm sauntering along sun-baked streets and am overtaken by a sudden urge to stop and say something, anything, or as I try to recall a particular dream that I feel is important but can't seem to recall – which is to say: when I feel the weight of how long it's been since I last saw you – I think of this house.

In the wind, the drifting snow soars above the rooftop.

And while dwelling on this landscape, I have ceased to know my age.

———

I am Naghi.

The na in Naghi is written 鎘, which means pot, specifically the lidded gamasot kind. I was to be named Naghil, in fact, but the last consonant was lost. That would be the ㄹ in 길. I wrote the ㄹ much too low, Mother said. It was Father who went to register my birth and who, drunk, read the last character as ghi, not ghil, shuffled though the Hanja dictionary, and lighted on the first Hanja for ghi he found. Likewise with na: he'd flipped through, found the relevant page, and, pointing a finger, copied down the first character he saw. When she found out, Mother was livid; but with the hours she had to pull at the market couldn't find a moment to go and undo what he'd done, and so by default I became Naghi. In the end, it hardly matters. Once a teacher did ask me why my parents had ever thought to give their child such a name, which made me pause for thought, but after rifling through the Hanja dictionary I realised there weren't that many Hanja for na with a good meaning in any case. I am Naghi. And this suits me fine. As long as I consider it a witty contribution by my drunken father, the name's fine by me. A vessel made of cast iron.

Naghi's na is written 鎘, which means gamasot.

The ghi 其 is possibly the unit of measurement for pots; there's no particular meaning attached to it. And

I say that's fair enough as definitions go.

—

In the night, the ground shook.

Feeling dizzy, I awoke. I was in the grip of a slow, ponderous force that tugged heavily at me. An earth-quake: distantly the thought gathered shape, as though itself an extension of sleep. There was an underground line not far from here, but no trains would be running at this time. Except, perhaps, the odd empty carriage on a late-night run along subterranean tracks, but no, the real source of the rumblings seemed to lie much deeper.

Slowly I roused myself. It was dark. Nana was asleep. Sora and Mother, too. I could hear them breathing. The heat from the day still lingered, I could smell the sour tang of boiled green bean sprouts, and pork, and the dough turning. Another huge batch of mandu this year. It wouldn't fit in the fridge, so we had to dig out every tray we could find and lay them out all over the living room. By first light, half of them would need to be thrown out. Mother will be dismayed. It's all food, this, we could've eaten it instead of letting it go to waste if only we'd had enough mouths around, she'd say wistfully. The food bin will have to be packed full of mandu. It's no use suggesting we try to make a bit less since there aren't enough of us to eat it all: every year it's the same. I wonder if she does this just to show me, if insisting on making more mandu than we can handle is her way of belabouring a point. A silent reproach implying that it's my refusal to expand the family that leads to all this waste.

For it is my mother's fervent wish to become a grandmother.

She'd grown up lonely after losing her family at an early age, and she dreams of the bustle of grand-children, but I am unable to realise this dream for her. Until fairly recently she used to ask me, in chiding tones, if there wasn't any nice woman I was seeing, but lately she's stopped needling me with questions about my romantic life. I'm not asking for a daughter-in-law, all I want is to see you bring me a baby somehow, she used to say, but not these days. She may have given up, or perhaps she hasn't, not yet, and is in fact being strategic by withholding comment. More likely the latter, I say, she's probably holding on to some remnant of hope. It saddens me to watch her grow old without seeing such a modest wish fulfilled.

I feel along the table with its oil bottle, salt pot, rubberbanded flour pack until my fingers find Mother's cigarette pack. Borrowing a fag, I head out the door and am surprised to see it's lighter outside than in.

The sun will be up soon. I light the cigarette and look down the alley. The cracked egg-yolk yellow stains are still visible in the street out front. That's where Sora and Nana and the man called Moseh got into a brawl earlier. There is no sign of eggshells. A street cat would have licked them clean. Yesterday was the first time I'd laid eyes on the man called Moseh. I'd gone out to see what the commotion was about, and saw Sora and Nana and that man knotted up in a bizarre tangle. Literally had to prise them off one another. Even more than Nana, Sora was the one who was all worked up and livid. Yelling something I couldn't figure out, she wouldn't quit pouncing on the guy, it was as if she'd turned into a human spring. My hands still smart from trying to pull her off the man. Nana's man, Moseh ssi, was sweating profusely. Shirt and shoes soaked through. Finally Nana told him to leave and he left, but he's not likely to give up. I could recognise it in him. He won't give up. Recalling his indescribably contorted face, I take a long drag. His is an unfamiliar face that isn't at all unfamiliar. This makes me detest him. And pity him. How wretched. And yes, deplorable. The site of my old wound starts to throb. The wound that's no longer there. I breathe in; my throat is instantly parched. I smoke only very rarely.

I've limited it to these rare occasions. Not because I cook for a living, or because I worry how smoking might dull my tongue and affect the food I make, or because I have qualms about handling food with nicotine-stained fingers.

No. This is your smell.

And it must remain your smell.

If I smoke any more than I do now, this smell that is your smell would become my smell.

I'd lose the sole reason I have for smoking.

I watch the smoke until it dissolves in long streaks into the emptiness. There's a scent of apple.

It's the scent of you.

You were small. With wispy hair and red lips. You were rude. You were violent – and quiet. You'd explode into fits of laughter sometimes, no one could figure out why. When you burst out laughing like that, not every time but some of the time, I felt I'd lose it completely. Your eyes were set slightly apart, and tended, slightly, to gaze in different directions. Your pupils were very yellow. They were eyes that convinced. Eyes that made your actions, at their tamest and their most violent, somehow acceptable, made one feel that it wasn't surprising for a person with such eyes to behave that way, that's how peculiar they were. But in truth, I don't know. Had I wanted to hit you. Or touch you. Had I wanted to throttle you. Or had I wanted to touch you. I wait for you. Wait for news of you. But which is it, news of life or news of death. Which am I waiting for. Lately I've told myself, on more than a few occasions, that it must be your death I'm waiting for. I am no longer able to distinguish whether it's you or your death I await.

I can't tell any longer.

That's how long it's been.

It's been too long since I saw you.

—

The tremors that shook me out of sleep tonight, perhaps they also roused you from sleep, perhaps you felt them too. Perhaps they made their way across the sea to where you are, these seismic waves that rise up from a place deeper and more intimate than the surface of the earth. Or perhaps they reached me from wherever you are now. This night may have convulsed because the place where you are convulsed. Where are you? Could you still be there? The city I was in several years ago, in that country where earthquake warnings are a regular occurrence - could you still be there? And was it there that quaked tonight?

The tremors must have been substantial to have made it this far. People there must have heard the thunderous noise rippling through the air. Lights must have swung from ceilings, knick-knacks spilled off shelves onto floors. For years now they'd been saying a great earthquake was imminent there, so with the first vibrations people would have been even more alarmed than usual. Then, while the series of after-shocks followed, they would have feared that these were the precursors to the great earthquake. But by and by they would have calmly returned to routine, as though there was nothing else they could do.

What's become of that small room, I wonder.

That dark, unheated room.

With its tatami mats that were stained and scummy and sour with rot. In that wooden building, there were sixteen of these rooms replicating in succession hori-zontally then mirrored vertically on the second floor. The custodian was a middle-aged woman whose throat rattled with phlegm every time she spoke, and she looked on those of her boarders who didn't speak her language – Chinese, Korean, Indonesian – with suspicion. Cooking on the premises, including indoors, was forbidden on the grounds that foreign-ers, who made up the bulk of her tenants, were prone to start fires. Any chance she'd get she'd lurk outside your door, or knock on your window pretending to see how you were doing, all so she could monitor the use of any sort of burner in the room. Fluorescent lights and heating were non-existent in the building, one had to make do with a small lamp in summer and rely on the light of an electric heater for additional illumination in winter. Winters and summers were equally brutal in that room. During my stay in that country I passed through several rooms in a state similar to that one, but even so, that room remained unique. Not for being particularly harsh, but because that was the room where you came to visit me. You stayed a fortnight in that room.

—

I'd met you when I was fourteen. Physically smaller than me and fairly unexceptional in the way you spoke and behaved, you were the boy who showed up to class with bruises pretty regularly.

Both your parents were educators. Your father taught English at a private high school and your mother was a primary school teacher. You attended the school your mother taught at. For six years your teachers were also colleagues of your mother's. For a long time, you were known as the teacher's son instead of by your own name. It was the rare person who didn't know this, and when you went on to the neighbouring secondary school things were no different. Anyone who knew you knew of your parents, and for that reason alone there was an oddly quiet attention paid to you. Mostly you remained as unexceptional as ever, but anytime you did say or do something all eyes seemed to turn to you, as if to say, his mum's a teacher, isn't she, and his dad too – so went the pattern.

Once I saw you intentionally checking your speed in a hundred-metre race.

You seemed to take special care not to stand out. To remain an unobtrusive part of the crowd as much as possible, to neither excel nor lag behind in your studies and at sports. One day the Korean teacher cracked a joke in class and asked if anyone knew how to say toothpaste in English – this at a time when most students didn't encounter English or its grammar until secondary school. *Toothpaste*, I heard you answer as if without thinking, and I and everyone else turned round to stare at you, all of us surprised by your hollow, brusque pronunciation. You ducked your head, flustered, and never repeated anything of the sort ever again.

Your father was not a kindly teacher. It was rumoured that to his children in particular, he was an even harsher disciplinarian than he was to his pupils. And as if to prove the rumour well-founded, every so often, just as we were about to forget, you would show up to school with bruises on your chin, or your eyes, or arms, or ears.

It was near the end of the brief winter that marked the beginning of the term. Every Monday our class switched seats according to a complicated system of seat rotation, and on that particular Monday, you and I wound up sitting one behind the other. You were taking notes, I was sitting with my chin resting in my hand. A sheet of paper was taped on the blackboard – a large drawing of a rice flower – and the Biology teacher was explaining the pollination process of rice plants. An anemophilous flower: the pollen is dispersed by wind. No honey and no scent, its fertilisation straightforward, fuss-free, and involving only wind-borne pollen.

The back of your neck was a deep violet.

The purple bruise plumed from behind your left ear like a cockscomb flower, extending down the nape to vanish into the collar of your top.

He's bruised again, I said to myself.

I was sitting there transfixed when you raised your left hand and started scratching your neck. The nails scraped skin, and then you covered the spot with your palm. Your thumb and forefingers were hidden beneath the folded collar, I could only see your ring and little fingers. How far did that bruise extend? The contrast of bruise and flesh was vivid, and the slender ring finger was gingerly pressing the area as if to trace the boundary of the two. I watched until I felt my face flush. I found the bruise pretty, and sensual. I didn't even know what sensual meant back then, all I remember is the feeling of frustration that I didn't have the words to express what I felt. I wanted to see the rest of the bruise that snaked inside your collar, I wanted to lay the palm of my hand on your back.

I was intrigued.

I wondered about the shape of your back.

I wondered how it would feel, would it be soft?

What about the rest of you.

Would it feel rough?

Would you be hot or warm against my hand?

If I told you I wanted to look at you, and touch you, with what expression would you look at me?

How near you would I be able to get?

Would this much be alright? Or this much?

What about this much?

I wonder why the top of your head looks the way it does. Why your ears are the way they are. Could I reach out and feel them? Would it be alright? To touch your neck as you do? That habit you have of touching the neck, are you even aware of it? Are you aware how poignant, how wrenching it is to see you do that? And your other habits, of looking off into space before speaking, of leaning all your weight on one elbow even with both arms on the desk, of fingering the ear of a page when you read – are you aware of these habits? Every single one of them? I wanted to talk to you about these habits of yours. Why do you do that? Why this? I wanted to ask you about every single one of them, and hear you answer.

—

How did it start?

I had asked you something.

You'd replied no.

Then I'd asked again, and after a while you said yes.

You turned around to face me and you spoke to me, and though I couldn't show it, this made me ecstatic with joy. You spoke about your father. About how he was always telling you to join the ranks of the elite. A real man must live the life of a judge, a prosecutor, a doctor. For that you should by now have shown promise, but as far as he could tell you weren't remotely close to showing the germ of such potential. That was the gist of what he said to you, that you didn't have it in you and would therefore live a pitiful life. You repeated your father's words to me with a gruff, convoluted look on your face, then asked about my father, asked me what he was like. You were asking me how my father treated me. When I said he was dead, you asked how he had died.

How had he died?

I didn't know much about my father. I knew he'd been timid when sober and fearless when not, and that was pretty much it. I told you the story as it had been told to me. My father suffered a heart attack and collapsed while working at the market one winter. He was carrying a full rack of apple crates on his back when this happened. The apples tumbled out and scattered every which way, while a heap of sawdust obscured his head. The other vendors had no way of gauging what state his neck was in under all those crates, the most they could do was remove the crates and leave him as he was. One of them later told my mother that she'd been surprised by how warm the apples were, once they finally lifted him into the ambulance – the apples that had lain squashed under him felt surprisingly warm – and it made my heart sink, to think what a sorry life he'd had, the woman said, extending her sympathies to my mother at the funeral hall – and this was the tale I repeated to you.

You seemed most interested in how my father

had harassed people at the market every time he got drunk, then had fallen to his death and was now gone. It was your desire for intrigue and revenge that drove your appetite for this story. I was fully aware of this. I knew which parts of the story you found most satisfying, and though this realisation chilled me, I was far too enamoured by the way your eyes bore straight into mine not to repeat the story to you again and again. Thus my father's death became a story of cause and effect: he had suffered punishment – for being a drunk and for inflicting mayhem to those around him, he had met a miserable end. We related the story back and forth until it became increasingly unclear which of us had started telling it, and in this way we wound up rewriting the ending to my father's life as we saw fit. It was a scathing tale, one I myself would rather have believed over the truth. And yet recalling the story when I was alone, I'd be wracked by shame. Seeing the exhaustion on my mother's face at night, knowing she'd been working all day in the precise spot where my father had met his death, I was tormented by guilt. Nonetheless the next time you demanded the story, I would tell it to you. Willingly, too.

Whatever and whenever.

If you desired it, I was ready to do it.

—

As summer deepened you became increasingly venomous. You fell in with a bad lot, joining in on their pastime of marking out and devouring easy prey as fancy dictated. The type of people that consider such savagery plain good fun. They'd hone in on a target, smile ingratiatingly as they borrowed a biro, a notebook, a textbook, the chair, the trainers, the uniform. The 'borrowing' gathered force incrementally until the victim reached a point where even the things he couldn't afford to lend had to be loaned out; they would demand of him, purely for the sport of it, everything he owned. C'mon, let us borrow it. Just the once. That's all. Just the once, I swear. But the borrowed things wouldn't be returned, or hurled back, until they had been picked apart and destroyed. And when, for instance, it came time for their latest mark to speak in turn during class, they'd kick up a racket, thumping on desks and laughing exaggeratedly. All purely in jest, of course; albeit the sort of jesting that disallows whoever must bear the brunt of it from earnest objection, and can only end in heartache.

You started referring to your father as that shit, not caring who heard you. That shit became that prick, which became dickwad: dickwad beats the crap out of me every day, I wish he'd drop dead, the shit, the fucking prick, same goes for the fucking cow. You started showing up to class after a few sips of alcohol, or you'd smuggle it inside your bag. You seemed to consider having a nip a handy way of faking sick, since the flush in your face made the pretend-fever more plausible. On these days, you'd spend the entire morning assembly slumped over your desk, ears and forehead a bright red, then go home before afternoon classes started. To avoid getting collared at the school gates, you needed a permission slip with a teacher's signature; you would order me to go to the homeroom teacher and explain how poorly you were, get the teacher to sign the slip. And I'd do as I was told. I was forever watching you, and the moment you turned to me and demanded something, anything, of me, I acquiesced.

Perv.

That was what those gang pricks called me. Hey, perv. Once in a while they'd drag me out to the incinerator behind the school grounds. Why you gotta stare all day?

You find something funny?

You find us funny?

You want a real laugh?

I was dragged along a narrow path that reminded

me of the hundred-metre track. Scraggly ginkgo trees and a fence covered in blue-black moss cast shade over the entire length of it. Where the path reached its end there was a roofless makeshift structure of cement bricks. This was the incinerator; after they banned the burning of trash, it had fallen into disuse and was now abandoned. A pile of gingko leaves were heaped against the sooty inner walls, partially burnt plastic and woody remains from the last incineration lay scattered from however many years ago. The utility of the incinerator was long lost, but its four walls still reeked of burnt sugar, and ash lay stagnant on the ground. And right there, that's where I would kneel, or break my fall with the flat of my palms, or slobber as I lay on my side, or throw up gastric juices. I kneeled because I was made to kneel, I rolled because forcibly rolled about. Those sons of bitches beat and kicked at me with fists and feet from any direction, and in whatever manner they felt like, with a deep hatred for the body they were laying into. They would have hated my body for being vulnerable, for being beaten up, and the more they lashed out the more their revulsion would have grown, making them strike out with even more force. No matter how many blows I endured, it seemed the situation would never reach an end.

You did not intervene, ever. You neither participated nor prevented. Instead you'd sit flicking through magazines on a partially burnt sofa. I would watch you. Even through the beatings I watched you as I always watched you. I watched in desire and with resentment, cursing you for not throwing me a single glance even now.

I couldn't understand it.

Why was I being beat up by these shits and not by you.

It should be you.

You should be the one fucking me up.

You're the only one.

It should have been you.

When I approached you, you lifted your head and looked at me. Your face was pale and untouched and the complete reverse of my own, now smeared with crushed leaves, ash, and dirt. Blood seeped in through my swollen, busted lips. It was salty, and it stung. But this pain meant nothing to you. I couldn't forgive myself for suffering a pain that meant nothing to you. Anger rose up in me. It's unfair, I thought. Meaning what, what was unfair? This I didn't know exactly, but it was nonetheless horribly unfair. The next minute I was kicked behind the knee. I collapsed to the floor; immediately I got up. I seized your arm as if to wrest it from you, and that's when you looked at me.

With those yellow eyes.

You laughed as if to say, how absurd.

A blow to the head knocked me out.

—

Listen, Nana says.

Am I selfish.

Am I. Because that's what Moseh ssi said. He said
I'm selfish. He asked me why I don't consider the
social damage and so on to the child. And it's true, I
don't think I am considering it, or not as much as I
should be. I thought I'd be fine no matter what people said, but maybe the reason I felt confident was
because I hadn't thought enough about it. Maybe this
resolve, being determined to see this through on my
part only leaves the baby vulnerable, gives the baby
no choice other than to bear life and endure pain? I
mean, what with the rest of the world being how it
is, and how tongues will wag. In fact, even the world
and what it is, all that has to be considered from a
new perspective, doesn't it. And how is it, the world?
Fine, is it? Fit enough that I can bring a child into
it? What if the baby asks me why I let it be born?
Look, the average lifespan these days is about eighty
years, right. What if in all that time there's nothing
but misery? What if the baby, born because of me,

spends thirty, forty years of its life being plain miserable? What if it regrets being born? No matter how much you weigh and consider beforehand, there's still all this other stuff to think about, isn't there. So I want to, I want to think more on it, but when I do then I have to also think about whether it's right or good to spend so much time thinking so deeply in the first place. Listen, how does everyone manage it. How do people make babies at all, in fact? How do they dare have them? Is everyone thinking these same thoughts, being ever so conscientious, and all the while busily trying to make a baby? Are they all tirelessly considering all this, in fact, with as much fervour as they can muster, and only afterwards, once they've reached a decision resolving to have and raise a child?

—

Zig, zig, zig, zig.

Nana says that's how the baby's heart moves.

That it's more sensation than sound, more a sensing, than hearing, of the frantic beating of muscle towards the tail end of her spine.

Zig, zig, zig, zig.

Since hearing her describe it in this way, I've found my thoughts dwelling increasingly on that little bundle of muscle. Zig, zig, zig, zig, I'll even catch myself murmuring as I've seen Nana do. Lately Nana has become accustomed to dropping in more frequently at the bar looking haggard. And she asks difficult questions to which I have no answer. All I can do is listen, and smile impotently. What could I have to tell her. Aren't I waiting for you? Waiting only for you? But what exactly do I await? I wait for news that will tell me that you live, or that you are dead. For the end of the world, or something like it. No longer able to tell whether it's you or your death I wait for, I find myself considering my own death as I consider yours, and the end of the world. So how could I respond, how am I to respond to a question concerning the state of the world, whether it's fine enough or fit enough?

Is it fine?, Nana asks, almost as if to herself, but I don't have an answer, either.

Was my being born a good thing?

Zig, zig, zig.

Zig, zig, zig, zig.

What is it like, to sense such a thing with your body. My mother would have experienced it too. The resounding zig, zig, zig. And what was the result of it but me, who amounts to a pot, absurdly enough – at this thought I erupt in laughter. A long, hard laugh that brings tears to my eyes, and leaves me empty and bereft. I am Naghi. And how did my mother fare after giving birth to me. Was my being born a good thing.

I don't know my mother as a woman living a woman's life. I know her as someone who labours: out in the streets, exposed to the elements without decent shelter from the wind, face darkened, selling her wares. Her voice not once outmatched by the men about her as she calls to passers-by and refuses to back down from an argument. Each night collapsing into sleep as if she'd been knocked out, like she'd never wake again, except she would, unfailingly, and head out the door each dawn with a towel wrapped around her neck. My working mother, with her ten numbed fingers. Mother's womanhood was cut short early on. To imagine that she has in fact, unbeknown to me, had her share of decent sex – this cheers me up; I prefer to think that's the case. Since packing it in at the market, Mother has continued taking on odd jobs, saying she's not used to being at home. Lately she's been working as a cleaner at an officetel building near the subway, and she likes the blue uniform so much she's taken to leaving home in it in the mornings. It pains me a bit to see her enthuse over these things, and I ask her if it isn't time for her to take a break from work, but she says the work she does now is hardly difficult, especially compared to what she did before, and that it's actually quite comfortable. That it's warm in winter and cool in summer, which she finds very agreeable.

—

Today the man called Moseh stopped by Wage.

After the lone customer who'd sat poking at his capelin and drinking beer paid his bill and left, not a soul had set foot in the bar. I'd just about decided to close up for the day. Then the door slid open and a man stepped in quietly. Moseh, it was Nana's Moseh ssi. He stood and looked over at me, it seemed as if he'd been waiting for the bar to be empty of patrons. He appeared calmer than the last time I'd seen him, but also visibly drained. Setting down his black brief-case on the table, he settled into a chair. I wiped the chopping board with a dry towel and waited for him to speak.

Nana ssi drops by here sometimes, doesn't she?

He continued, I know she comes here to see you. Very often. Nana ssi won't talk to me these days. I don't know what the issue is. Here I am, burning with my ardent feelings for her, but Nana ssi is cold and indifferent. I can't approach her even at work. Since the other day I've…, he trailed off. His gaze fell to the edge of the table, and then he asked me, are you in love with Nana ssi?

In love?

Does Nana ssi love you?

I thought a while and then by way of answering said, Nana loves me as I love her. But I'd say it's a different sort of love from what you have in mind.

At this the man stared at me before asking, what sort of love is that?

He had a strange manner of looking at a person. Even when it seemed his gaze was directed this way, it was difficult to tell whether he was actually looking at you, you had to keep checking his eyes to see if he was. I wondered what sorts of conversations Nana would have had with a person like this, and in what sorts of places. He spoke again, slowly tilting his head. There is no love between a man and a woman that is not the love between sexes.

Even if it may not be the case now, when it comes to men and women, it's bound to come to that. Isn't that obvious?

Ajossi.

Ajossi, I repeated.

Don't erase things from the world just because you are incapable of imagining them.

—

For instance, there's this house.

A house that's difficult to imagine. A house that someone like you would say can't be imagined at all.

A house some people might easily dismiss into non-existence purely because they can't imagine it.

To speak about this house properly, perhaps one needs to enlist the help of images. It was that sort of a house. A single space that was also two spaces with a wall down the middle: split into left and right like the spread wings of a moth or a darkened decal, a half-basement on either side whose orientation shifts depending on where you're stood. Although it's only partially below ground level, apart from the lighter entrance area the house was so dark that even during the day you couldn't tell objects apart without keeping the lights on, and it was in this house that I spent a quiet childhood wordlessly letting my imagination roam free.

For as long as my mother and I lived in that house, the space across the wall saw a steady stream of tenants. Its occupants changed frequently, and for moderate to long stretches it would stand empty. People who did move in there were either never home or always home. In either case, these people never had much to say, and even when you ran into them at the entrance there was no indication of their having registered the presence of another person. Mother used to complain that they made a mess of the bathroom, regarding it not as their own but as someone else's. And it was in this house that I met Sora and Nana, and got to know their mother, Aeja Ajumoni.

When it comes to Aeja Ajumoni, my mother's thoughts seem to comprise a jumble of emotions, similar to the patchwork cloths she makes sometimes. She's close to atrocious as a mother, but pitiable as a person; she's pitiable as a person, but as a mother she's atrocious – I'd say these two statements more or less summarise the various flip-flopping emotions Mother feels towards Aeja Ajumoni. When Sora and Nana were still quite young, Aeja Ajumoni would go to the market or to the public baths with Mother, or else sit with us even if she didn't contribute much to the conversation. But over the years she became increasingly unwilling to interact with people, and gradually, and quietly, became a wreck. To say she became a wreck may not be the best way to describe her current state. To say she reached completion or achieved culmination would be the more appropriate way of putting it. Over a lengthy stretch of time, she has steadily, inaudibly, fulfilled her pain and become whole. She has hauled her pain over herself, covering herself entirely with it, like a carapace. Will there ever be an opportunity to speak about her, about her life, again? To tell the truth, in the beginning I didn't pay her or her daughters much mind. They'd simply materialised on the other side of the wall one day, and would just as suddenly dematerialise one of these days, I'd thought then, leaving me alone as always in that big, uncanny space. They were no different from all the rest who'd grazed past me with their awkward or unpleasant or gruff faces outside the bathroom we had to share.

Dokkebi.

That's how I regarded these people.

Walking about without a hint of a footfall or a word until the day they abruptly vacated the other side and vanished into thin air. Neighbours across the wall.

I used to wake up alone in the middle of the night, and then I'd step out of my room, past Mother's, and cross over, walk past the wall. Whatever the season, my back would always be damp with sweat on these nights. I'd stand with my back to the wall in the opposite hallway until the sweat had dried, and only then come back to bed. It's not that I found this fun or felt especially adventurous. Sometimes next door would be empty, sometimes not. In either case, I found it somewhat frightening. And maybe that was the reason I did it. Maybe what I needed was confirmation. Whether somebody was there or not, the silence and

the dark across the wall *were* scary, and maybe that's
why I found it necessary to witness this myself. Since
to leave it alone would make it even scarier; since
the more I dwelled on the fear, the more terrifying
it would in fact become, perhaps even forcing its way
over to where Mother and I slept. Even after Sora and
Nana and Aeja Ajumoni moved in, I went on with
my nocturnal confrontations, or attempts at dispelling
malice, for some time.

Sora and Nana had almost no possessions.

They'd moved in with barely any sign of life, so
I assumed whenever they moved out, it would be
the same. But the two sisters remain a part of my life
to this day, and by now this is what feels natural. So
natural that it seems wholly unnecessary to try and
pinpoint when exactly this change occurred.

Just as Sora and Nana are familiar with my childhood, I am familiar with theirs.

Dokkebi, I said, and the two girls blanched.

Did he say dokkebi?

This house has dokkebi?

Behind the small girl the even smaller girl hid herself. Nana was terrified, and Sora, no doubt just as
terrified as Nana, pretended otherwise and stared at
me. Two scrawny, sad, lonely little girls. I've never
actually told them, so Sora and Nana probably have no

idea how delighted I was in that moment, as delighted as any mischievous kid. How childlike in my glee and overjoyed I was, and how precious that moment felt to me. The sisters are all grown now but for all I know are still afraid of dokkebi, and in a few months a baby will be born, a baby who resembles them.

And this man is the father of that baby.

———

Is it fine?

I wiped the knife with a dry towel and laid it on the chopping board.

Ajossi, I called, making sure his eyes were focused on me. Addressing the eyes, I said, don't ever lay a hand on Nana again. If you do, Sora will not forgive you. And I will not forgive you. If you so much as lay a finger on her again, you will taste a bitter truth.

That bitter taste of realising that forgiveness will never be granted.

You will learn the taste of this.

———

Does Nana love me?

Nana loves me, yes. She has for a long time. She's tried all manner of ways to make me see it. Like a duckling, was how I saw it. That it was akin to the impetuous tagging along of a duckling that's attracted to whatever it lights on the moment it hatches. Imprinting, as they call it. But when I tried to convince her of this, Nana burst into tears. I was brought up short. Nana had never been one for crying. I've only ever seen her cry three times. I hit her once; that was the first time. The second was when I explained about imprinting and then had no choice but to show her your photo because she started sobbing. The third time was when the guy called Moseh followed her all the way to the house.

Nana rarely cries, but when she does, it's with a booming wail. When she cries, she is transformed. The usual prim and plucky face is instantly replaced by the crumpled expression of a howling infant. But does it really amount to a transformation? Might that not be Nana's real face? Like the kernel that's only revealed when the husk is removed, perhaps that is her essence. Otherwise I can't think of a single reason I find this face not in the least unfamiliar. Since becoming pregnant, Nana's shell has been crumbling in parts: she may yet return to her essence; she may be restored to her pith and start crying more often than she has until now. A young woman who cries with the face of a baby, and her baby – what will the world be like for the pair of them? Will the world

treat them well? Treat them kindly? Will it look lov-
ingly on them?

Do you love Nana?

Nana is loveable.

Nana is loveable and I am calculating. It may
be that I find Nana loveable because of her feelings
towards me. If so, it can't be helped. When someone
loves you to that degree, you can't help but find the
person loveable.

Would you have agreed?

Did you ever find me loveable?

—

We went on to high school, and I continued to seek
you out. I hovered, always on the lookout for you.
You remained outside the school walls as if there was
nothing of interest left within them now. You had a
gaggle of girls with you, always, and rode a motor-
cycle with a mantis-like raised seat. Strange stories
concerning you and your lot swirled about. That you
took turns doing it with girls in noraebangs, that you'd
got high sniffing glue in a rooftop room somewhere
(so they'd all be passed out, yeah, and then there'd
be this knock, except when they opened the door
there'd be no one there so they'd close the door and
come back in, but then there'd be this loud thudding

and stamping from the ceiling, and they'd yell what the fuck!, and it'd go all quiet, but the next morning when they came outside there was this pair of shoes, no idea whose, just lying there all neat like, while all the rest of their shoes had been flung down over the building, yeah), that you'd properly laid into a group of kids from some far-off school simply for rubbing you up the wrong way, and ended up blinding one of them.

I'd often see you sitting in a McDonald's with your gang and a map open in front of you. A map of where, I couldn't tell. The lower edge or side margin was a clean blue, so maybe some place by the sea. I worried that you'd go off somewhere far away never to return again, but after some time you always returned to the neighbourhood and to the school, and there would be moments when I'd even bump into you by chance while out walking in the evenings. You would be stood with the other boys, cigarette dangling from your lips, and always with your shoulders hunched as if you were cold no matter what time of year it was. Then when you did happen to notice me, you'd look squarely at me.

You shit.

In December, you spoke these words to me.

That December you would show up nearly every

day with bruises. Perhaps your father had knocked you about again or you'd been in a fight. And once in that same month, at a bus stop, you bumped into me. I'd been to the stationery shop and was just leaving with a new pen I liked. In the force of you brushing past me I stumbled, almost losing my balance; you looked at me with scorn as you took a couple of steps back, before turning and continuing on your way. That was all, and yet I was ashamed. Ashamed and angry with myself. That I'd been holding the new purchase in its pretty packaging so preciously in my hand, not to mention my neat get-up and the trainers I'd laced all the way to the top: all of this I found shameful – for being so mundane and safe, for being so far removed from you.

Then there was the incident, that same month.

That day I saw you in the school sports ground. My class was in the middle of a volleyball lesson.

I was scuffing the frozen sand with the soles of my trainers, when a group of kids not in their PE kits but in school uniform swarmed out. Having reached the sports ground they stood in a neat row and bowed their heads. A teacher strutted back and forth in front of them, a snooker cue in hand, then called on someone – you. It looked like he was asking you a question. He stood there stamping the ground with his cue stick, then with a sudden movement hurled it aside and struck you with his foot. You fell to the ground. You fell to the ground, and remained there, unmoving. Again I felt shame creep up on me. Crumpled there, you looked weak and pathetic. You were always sporting bruises, so I knew regardless of how many punches you yourself were landing or how the situation panned out, you often received blows yourself, but to see it happen with my own eyes beggared belief. I found it incredible that someone could transform you like that, in a mere instant. Get up, I willed with all my might. Get up. Get up, get up. I willed you to get right back up and do to the teacher what he'd done to damage you. I willed you to kick and punch his dull, thick waist, to spit in his brazen forehead. Get the fuck back up, I thought, get up, get up.

You got up. Picking yourself up like it was nothing you sauntered across the ground, and with a practiced hop disappeared over the fence.

—

I followed you. You wore no jacket or coat over your school uniform, and had flat slip-ons on your feet. There was sand on your back, and one of your shoelaces had come undone and was being dragged and trampled on with every step. I wanted to call to you, to run over to you and tie up your laces myself, and with this thought I continued to trail behind you. At the bus stop you got on the first bus that pulled up. You sat down at the far end of the rear seats, I at the other end. The driver grumbled that we hadn't paid the fare, but left us alone. My eyes felt parched in the dry air being blasted out from the heater right above me. The bus reached the midpoint of its route and turned round to head back, retraced the way it had come before finally pulling into the terminus, and all this while you remained unmoving in your seat. You remained seated, so I remained seated. People got on the bus, sat down between you and me, got off again. The further the bus travelled, the calmer I felt. People getting on and off the bus, the sound of fabric brushing past and of people moving about in their seats, the faces that seemed unrelated and yet alike, the endless loop of passengers stepping on and off, on and off; the bus trundling on, at times noisily, at times silently, straight ahead or round corners – and when making a turn the bus clearly slanted to one side, and I got to thinking that the long rear seat was like a see-saw, tilting first towards you, then towards me. I found myself hoping that at one point one of us might flow down towards the other; if we could sidle closer on this see-saw, so that we were nearer, seated right alongside... so I went on imagining, foolishly, as I gazed out the window. Sometimes I'd catch your reflection in the lightly frosted-over glass. Your breathing seemed to have eased since we'd first sat down. By the time we reached the terminus, the sun was setting. I followed you down the empty bus. An evening star floated in the reddened sky. You stood there for a minute as if pondering which way to go, before suddenly turning to me.

You, stop following me. You said this in a tone almost of relief, as if sloughing something off.

Stop following me, you shit.

You shit.

I couldn't get the words out of my mind. The warmth behind them: for swear word or not, they had been said kindly. After that day you did not return to school. I heard rumours about you. Some said you were holed up at home, others claimed that you had been spotted on your motorbike, driving out with your crew to some far-off place, and quite frequently, too – but among the contrary rumours were also stories of how you'd severely injured your mother and that she'd had to be taken to the emergency room, how you were getting ready to start your military service, and how, when asked whether you'd ever thought of killing your father, you had answered yes, yes, twice, how you'd then had to undergo two physical exams for military service, and how you'd left in the middle of the night after taking a baseball bat to all the glass at home and to the car that was registered in your parents' name. Then you actually vanished. I heard nothing more. After high school graduation, I didn't see you at all, not even by chance. How much time passed until the day I saw you again at that funeral hall, I'm not sure. Enough time to make such a reckoning entirely beside the point. And still I believed I would meet you again. Of course I did. That I might never see you again, this was too strange even to contemplate. Inconceivable, unimaginable. I would meet you; I was bound to, at some point or other. I never doubted this, and so from time to time I was able to forget you and get on with my life.

—

Mother recently finished the patchwork blanket she had been working on for Nana. She'd started it after hearing Nana was pregnant, had found the time here and there to piece it all together. Swatches cut from old bedding sewn together in a colourful blend of silk satin and quality cotton to create a surprisingly beautiful blanket. It's not meant for Nana, it's a gift for the baby, so for now I'm keeping it a secret, she said to me as she folded the blanket away in a drawer. And as for me, what do I have to give, what could I offer Nana and her baby? This is what preoccupies me lately.

The dream recurs with increasing frequency these days, too.

It's a silent, entirely soundless dream, and yet it feels like a nightmare.

It's been too long since I saw you.

—

With increasing frequency, I wake up in a sweat in the middle of the night. Summer is at its end. The leaves have turned; the temperature, too. At night the air is chilly, I can't sleep with the windows open any more. At Wage a steady stream of people have started dropping in for something warming on their way home. Sora and Nana regularly stop by for a daily bowl of soup. Mother says when it's fully autumn she will visit her grandfather's grave as she did last year. When I mention this, Nana begs to be allowed to come with us this year. It's in the mountains, it'll be too tough, I try to dissuade her. So I'll climb slowly, she retorts, pouting. Nana is at Wage every day now. Sora is, too. Every day Sora goes to meet Nana outside her office, and the two of them stop at the bar before going home. I wish Nana would quit her job, Sora says. It's where that man is, isn't it, I wish she'd quit that place and find another job, she says. Nana pretends not to have heard this, and continues eating the braised potatoes I've put in front of her. Her lips are chapped, her complexion dull. She looks as if she's maybe put on a bit of weight and that's all, but a closer look at her belly will tell you she's pregnant. You okay?, I ask. Why shouldn't I be?, she retorts. Listen, she says.

Listen to this first. I heard some of my colleagues talking at work today. They're all women, all married, and today they were having a chat about how one of them got lucky in the housing lottery. But right next to this particular apartment complex are these SH Corporation flats, which apparently offer permanent rental housing. And so this one colleague, she was having doubts about moving into the area. It was a source of concern for her. It's poor people who tend to live in housing like that, she said, so there's bound to be all sorts of violence and crime and so on occurring around the neighbourhood, not to mention the number of saetomin, the North Korean asylum seekers, bound to be living there too, and of course the place would be swarming with single-parent households, and she did so hate the thought of her own children mixing with kids brought up that way. Children from single-parent homes can't but suffer from lack of parental care, which clearly leads to developmental differences. So for instance those children tend to be emotionally unstable, inarticulate, academically medi-ocre, and generally deficient. She said she worries about the effects on her own children of living side by side with these unhealthy kids. But – do you think it's true? Do you think it's really the case? Because am I not a single parent now? Am I not about to be a single parent? Does that mean my baby will grow up to be deficient? Will my child grow up unloved and unhealthy, because I'm a single parent – this is what's got me worried now.

Don't pay it any thought, Sora responds. Mindless talk like that. They're the unhealthy ones.

And what if it's not a single-parent household, is that enough then? A child with two parents will sup-posedly absolutely be loved, and absolutely grow up to be healthy? And those women, I suppose they're stood round worrying about these things because not one of them was raised by single parents and therefore they're, what, the paragon of health? Well, if that's what being healthy means, I'm fine with not being healthy. And it's fine if you're not healthy either.

But I *want* to be healthy.

Then think about what it means to be healthy.

Really think about it, Sora says. You've got to think, properly. Listening to Sora say these words I feel a strange sense of dissonance. Why is that, I ask myself, then realise that these are Nana's words, this is Nana's habitual phrase.

Sora's starting to sound like Nana now, I say. The sisters look up as one to stare at me. They're alike: two sisters becoming like with age. Is that what brothers or sisters do, start to resemble each other the more they age? But they do – they are. They're really alike, I think to myself, and then burst out laughing. The sisters look at me in confusion.

I say Nana's pretty healthy already, Sora mutters. I'd say Nana's far healthier than the lot of them, whatever anyone says. Nana's healthy. And I'm proud: proud of Nana, proud of me, proud of Naghi. Since if what they say is true, Nana and I and Naghi, well, we all grew up with single parents, didn't we. But we managed, we got this far, didn't we.

But yes, of course, I think. We were all raised by single parents, weren't we.

I'm completely taken aback by this.

Well, yes, obviously, we were raised by single parents. But it's not something I usually think about, so I hadn't realised.

While the two sisters carry on quietly eating their

food, I turn towards the window. A few drops of rain splatter down the glass pane. Nana asks for more braised potatoes and wolfs down another half-bowl of rice.

Nana's not as picky about soy sauce dishes now, Sora says.

Was I picky before?

You were.

You hated it, I say.

You were the tribe that hated soy sauce, Sora says. Nana looks at her as if to ask what on earth she means. But Sora sits there unfazed, like it was just an offhand remark. I'm astonished. I had no idea Sora still remembered. Twice tonight I've been taken by surprise. Twice bowled over, but offhandedly, like it was nothing at all.

—

Single-member tribes do exist in this world, you know.

I'd said something to this effect to Sora. A long while ago, before I'd left for Japan. The night before my departure, in fact.

The tribe that hates soy sauce.

The tribe that likes soy sauce.

The tribe that's indifferent to it.

How can it be a tribe, Sora had asked, when there's

only one of me?

Single-member tribes do exist in this world, you know.

It was one of those nights when no matter how much you drink, you simply can't get drunk. Sora and Nana were also at it, matching me glass by glass as if determined to keep up with me, until Nana eventually dozed off, leaving only Sora and me. Sora, Nana, Naghi, I said out loud, and marked three dots of water on the table.

But Naghi's too small, how come you're so tiny, you're the smallest of the three, I don't like that, Sora complained and started adding drops of water to it, one at a time, until it seeped and fused with the other two drops. The three separate drops merging to form one larger drop.

Shit, Sora had said.

Game over.

They're dead now.

Nana and I and Naghi, all dead, she said, eyes filling with tears as though she was genuinely torn up over it. A lorry rattled past outside. Sora peered down at the drop of water for a long, long while, her chin on the table. Then she said, they're not dead.

They've combined. Like the Power Rangers, three become one. Look at the shape of it, what do you think it looks like? I think it looks like, like…

Like a butterfly.

Not a moth?

Are moths better?

I don't know the difference, honestly.

Butterflies fly during the day, but moths fly at night. Which is better?

What if they flew in the day and also at night?

But that would be exhausting.

Even so, it could exist, a thing that flies both in the day and in the night.

I suppose.

Then that's what this is. Let's say that's what it is, a thing that flies at all hours of the day. At night as well as day – but what is this exactly, what do we call it?

Shall we name it?

Yeah. But it needs to have both butterfly and moth in the name – a combination of nabi and nabang!

Alright, a combination of nabi and nabang, then.

Nabangbi, Nabibang.

Nanabi.

Nabiba.

Nabiba sounds good.

Nabiba it is, then.

Nabiba.

When Sora, Nana, and Naghi combine, they

become Nabiba.

Yes, then we are Nabiba.

Sora Nana Naghi Nabiba.

Is it dead or is it alive?

It's alive.

It's Nabiba.

Sora Nana Naghi Nabiba.

All night we'd gone on like this, deep in an alcoholic haze.

A tribe of one.

———

You were the one who had mentioned the tribe of one. Back before I left for Japan. A month to the day prior to my departure, I received news of a death through the network of old school friends. I managed to remember his name: he'd been the carpenter's son, a former classmate who'd been in a motorcycling accident severe enough to permanently alter his face in high school – and he had been a member of your crew.

The funeral hall was twenty minutes away by taxi. Even before I got there, I knew I would see you. I could sense that you were there. I didn't think about the dead classmate, not even as a passing thought; you were all I thought of. I had to meet you, I told myself.

It was the second day of the wake and there were quite a few people who had come to pay their respects. As were you – you, sitting right at the back with three others, all of them former classmates of mine. Whether they recognised me or not I can't be sure, but I did recognise two of them. I sat down next to you at the low table. Bits of food streaked the disposable paper tablecloth; the bottles of alcohol were mostly empty. You seemed to recognise me, but the others didn't. Who are you? Well, who are you? When I answered that I was a classmate, they opened their arms wide and tried to hug my shoulders, their faces flushed with the booze, and dragged an empty shot glass in front of me. Aware of your mocking eyes on me, I accepted the soju that was offered and drank up without a word. My three former classmates, who'd once relieved their boredom by beating me up, now started to give an account of their lives and what they described as their mundane jobs – cram-school teacher, car park attendant, salesperson – cursing all the while. They cursed the world, they cursed death, they cursed the bland food, the peach-fuzz shits, the funeral hall, and the old farts, they raged against each other. Their rowdiness attracted fierce glares from the mostly subdued well-wishers. They were unwelcome friends. Which may be why they're raising hell in the first place, I thought to myself. From where I was seated I could see the framed photo of the deceased, buried amid the rows of chrysanthemums: the face of the man who used to so relentlessly and viciously attack me. At one point, you turned to me.

You must be pleased, you said.

No.

Heartbroken, are you.

No.

You pity him.

No.

Why'd you come then.

To see you.

You appeared somewhat leaner, smaller, and older. Your features were still that of a young boy's, and yet you looked very much aged. Your brute father was out of the picture by now, there was to be no more ageing for him.

Dead, last winter, you said. From cerebral haemorrhage when no one was home: momentary paralysis, convulsions, the end. Probably didn't even suffer that much. Unfair, that. Never did get around to patching it up, or making him see, or even getting payback for all the shite he pulled – quit before I even got started, the bastard. Croaked, didn't he. Left me all fucked up, the prick, buggered off on his own, free and unburdened. What I'd give to bash the life out of him, but he's gone and fucking died on me so can't do fuck-all, can I.

You told me all this as you downed glass after glass. You drank until you couldn't keep yourself upright, then you dozed off, nodding at the table full of food. At one point, with one big involuntary sway of the head, you knocked over a glass full of booze. Foamy beer instantly covered the table and streamed down into your lap. You jerked awake and watched in awe as the alcohol dripped from the edge of the table into your palms.

You see this. D'you know what this is. This is booze. This is life. *Life*. Spill it, and it's over. Spill it, and it's fucking *over*. Think you can catch it in the palm of your hand? Eh? Don't lie, don't fucking lie. You might be able to hold it a while, but not all the way. It'll stay put for a second, then it's gone. Where? Straight into air. Evaporated. But always, it leaves a mark. A filthy stain, dank and sour and filthy. And how's this different from a person? How are we any different, eh? Answer me, you shit. Don't we all croak? We like to think we're different, but it's all the same in the end, isn't it? You think you're different, you're not. Everybody goes. Thin air, poof. What's left? Extinction. I evaporate, I'm extinct. You evaporate, you're extinct. That prick, me, all extinct. This prick here, that one there, extinct. Babes in arms, drooling old sods, all wiped clean away. Can't be helped. What's that? Lonely? Yeah, you did. I heard you. Come out with it, fuckface, say it again, say it again, say you're lonely, I fucking dare you! Course you are. You're alone, how could you not be! Like a bloody tribesman in a fly-infested jungle, that's how alone I am. You think you're not? You think you're different? It's alright though. It's alright, it's all the same boat. All alone, all equally alone. A tribe of one. And then – gone. That's all. You, me, extinct, end of the line, blown into fucking oblivion, that's what...

You trailed off suddenly, staring wide-eyed down at your hand as if you'd had enough. You sat in complete silence, as though you hadn't been spilling a torrent of words a moment ago, and merely gaped, in complete, ponderous silence, at your beer-soaked palms. I fetched a wet towel and started wiping your hands. I ran the towel over your palms, the backs of your hands, the fingers, I flipped your hands and wiped them once more. You sat docilely through this. At times you'd blink slowly and open and shut one hand as if observing some curious, mystifying object, but you didn't retract either hand.

—

I asked you to give me your address. I said I'd send postcards.

I needed something concrete, I said, a street address that could be physically reached, as opposed to the email address or phone number that all but scatter away into the ether. At this you turned your bloodshot eyes at me, as if in silent laughter.

I remember it still.

The curve of your hand, the dip and swell of your palm. In which direction the middle phalange of your forefinger bent towards. All of this I remember, just as I remember how I longed to take that finger in my mouth. This sensory memory is a yearning, and will never be erased. If it is to be rubbed out, it will be the last memory to go. It will leave me only in my final moment.

With those hands you'll have received the postcards. The postcards I sent you. The cards with depictions of daruma, or neko, or Tokyo Tower, of the shades cast by cherry blossoms, of purple knots. I know that these postcards absolutely did make their way to you. Or at least one of them did. I know this because you came and found me at the address written on those cards. What did you do with them, I wonder. You will have thrown them out. You will have thrown them out or not thrown them out. Where are they now, those postcards.

Where are you.

—

Tonight Wage closes up a little after midnight. Sora is drunk. Nana hasn't been drinking but is also drunk. And I am drunk, too, though I've only drunk what was left in Sora's glass. Sora says there's someone at work who's been bothering her lately. Someone who's on her mind, making her uncomfortable, a real bother, she says. And as she talks she'll swing her fists up at the air suddenly, as if to erase something up there.

But I can't shake him from my mind, that's what's most annoying, she says. Remember how much it snowed last winter? Well, the night before Christmas, this guy was creeping along a snowy street when he saw another guy directly in front of him, a man in a big coat. This guy was also walking at a slow pace, real cautiously, because he was holding on to a cake box. To hand to his children with a big ta-da, I suppose, it being Christmas. How nice for those kids, he was thinking as he continued on, keeping his eyes on the other man. He envied the other man, he said. How happy the man's children will be, he thought, and how happy the man in turn. But as he was thinking this, the man ahead of him happened to slip and fall. He scrambled back up soon enough, but his coat was smudged with snow, and the man stood rooted to the spot, gaping down at the cake box, which was completely destroyed. And seeing that, he said, he found himself feeling as distressed as he imagined the other man to be. And what am I supposed to make of all this? I've thought about it, and I think that other man, the man he says he saw from behind, is in fact himself. He's talking about himself. But honestly, I've no idea why he's telling me these stories, Sora continues. It's annoying. It's really bothering me.

If it bothers you, isn't it because he gets to you, Nana says. Maybe it means you have feelings for him?

Sora scoffs at this and firmly shakes her head. That's not it at all, I just find him annoying. He won't stop talking to me about this stuff.

It's warm tonight, but as it's autumn, the air is forlorn with the smell of dried leaves. There's a general loneliness to the air, but at least we're headed home together. Making our way home as Nabiba, as one.

I wish we could go on walking, Nana says.

I want to walk on. Walk and walk until... where would we end up if we continued walking?

The sea.

And what do we do if we meet sea?

We cross it.

On foot?

Yes, on foot.

Nana's never crossed the ocean, actually.

Naghi has.

How was it?

How was it to cross the sea?

Sora and Nana ask me about my life there. What were the lodgings like. Did you like the tatami rooms. How does it feel to walk on tatami. How was the food. What are the high streets like. How were the people, and the earthquakes. What did you find beautiful, and what did you find scary there. They ask the questions they always ask, and I answer in the same way I always have. Tatami are tatami. The food was generally salty and didn't suit me. The high streets were full of people. I worked, ate, slept, and yes, felt the occasional earthquakes. I suffered from skin problems. People tend to develop skin problems when they're nutritionally deprived and under stress. People in the high streets were wary of Asians. When they figured out you were an Asian who didn't share their nationality, their faces would grow cold. There was an underhanded broker who tricked people. And a workplace that paid too little, and a Korean couple running a Korean-style restaurant who, when I protested the low wages, threatened to report my illegal status to the authorities.

What a couple of pricks, Nana says.

Yeah, they're pricks. And what else? What else was bad? And scary?

What did you find beautiful?

There was this one night when I came across a beautiful sight in one of the busier areas. It was the middle of the night and I was standing at a crossing, waiting for the light to change. Across the road there was a black wall encircling an old castle, and in front of the wall there was a man was playing the drums. I couldn't hear him, maybe because he was on the other side of the road. But there he was, drumming away with these big, intense movements, his head and upper body lurching with the beat. Since I couldn't hear anything it really looked like some type of performance art instead of just some guy playing music. The people next to me were entirely unmoved, though, they just stood there either looking or not looking in his direction. It was altogether odd, from the lone guy, the drums, the place, to the people and their indifference. But I found it beautiful. I thought it was beautiful.

I found the same scene frightening, too, in a way.

How those drums couldn't be heard despite how

powerfully he was beating on them.

How no one seemed to find the weird madness of this at all extraordinary.

—

After I'd found a place to stay and obtained an address, I started sending you postcards.

Sometimes I would leave the card blank, other times I'd scribble down a line or two.

It's raining.

Tokyo shook today.

Here they call chitterlings horumon. It's my job to transport horumon.

Some punks threw cans at me today, and laughed like oni.

Oni means dokkebi.

Found a potted plant.

The potted plant I mentioned in my last postcard had its first bloom last week.

Rain again. Rain in Japan is lukewarm and clammy. I've caught a cold.

Occasionally I'd write longer passages:

Standing at a bus stop one night, I saw a woman walk past with a girl of about seven. They seemed to be in a hurry, judging from their gait. A man was walking towards them from the opposite direction, and his bag brushed against the woman's arm as they passed each other. The man got angry. He was middle-aged, and wore a suit and tie. The woman said she was sorry, but he raged at her, swearing and cursing. The woman apologised at first, but eventually lost her temper, too, and started shouting back at the man. The man kept calling her baba, and shouting shi'ne. Kuso baba, shi'ne. At that the little girl stood in front of the woman and started arguing back at him. Shi'ne, shi'ne, she yelled sharply at the swearing man, in her cute red hooded jacket.

Shi'ne, shi'ne. Drop dead.

Either way, you never once wrote back.

I had known you wouldn't, but after moving to a new address, I continued to visit the old address on foot anytime I had a day off to check for post. Sometimes I'd be spotted as I stood and rifled through the envelopes, and before I knew it I'd be making a run for it, and on one such occasion I heard a voice behind me shouting sutohkah, sutohkah. *Stalker.* That sound stuck to the back of my head and wouldn't let go even after I'd half-run, half-tumbled headlong down the entire length of the slope, and this made me burst out laughing for some reason. Back in my room I kept repeating sutohkah, sutokah to myself, laughing until my sides creased from pain, until the pain got to be so much I had to roll over and lie with my cheek to the floor, panting, before the laughter erupted out of me again.

I didn't laugh, though, when a postcard finally did arrive from you.

You wrote to say you'd be crossing over here shortly, and would like to stay at my place for a brief while. The handwriting was messy, scribbled without care. I checked the date sent: ten days ago, and the date you were to arrive was another month away. Then the day rolled around, and there you were at my door.

Summer was drifting into autumn when you came, so yes, it was right about this time of year. You had one bag slung on your shoulder, and you stood and peered up at the ceiling of the shabby room. The cropped stub of an electrical wire jutted out where a fluorescent light should have been. You looked up intently at this, while I stared at you, in complete disbelief at your presence. Until that very morning you were not, and now you were. Here, in this room. Should I believe it? Could I? This wasn't Korea, even, but Japan, I told myself incredulously as I scratched an elbow that didn't itch. You, here, in this room. How did this happen. However it happened, you are, in this moment, here. You dropped your bag by the door and looked over at me. It's only for a short while, I won't stay long. I couldn't answer, merely nodded my head.

You told me you had come to make some money. But you had to meet up with someone first. A distant relative, someone who I gathered worked in the pleasure quarters. During the day when I was out working, you slept in that room, and would go out in the evenings only to return in the small hours or the next morning. I left a small light on by the door, a reading lamp with a red enamel shade. Small as it was, there wasn't a corner of the room that escaped its light. Even with my eyes closed, I could feel my optic nerves respond to the direction of the light. I'd turn my back on it and still be unable to sleep. Where would you be now. How near were you. Were you on your way back to this room. Would you return today. Could today be the day you didn't return.

Whether or not you found the person you'd come in search of, I don't know. You continued to return under cover of dark to the room, and shout that it was too dark in here, you blasted the room, and me along with it. This room stinks, you railed. It stinks from the ceiling, the walls, even the door handle is foul! And you, you reek, too! Unbelievable, the stench of it! And fucking tiny! Tiny! You'd rage and rage from the tatami floor, lying there without a blanket, before drifting off to sleep.

The final time I saw you, it was much the same. You came back close to dawn, all roughed up. Your left eye swelled shut, the skin above the brow gashed open and scarlet. Lips dotted with blood, chin stained black and blue. You looked a mess, and unusually despondent. I held you by the hand and sat you down, examined your wounds. Cleaned with a moistened towel the parts that needed cleaning, applied salve where salve was needed. When my fingers touched your chin you looked up. You didn't back away. You remained still. You let me continue. I took a step closer. I stopped. I approached, stopped again, approached, paused, approached again, and then I put my lips to your chapped lips. You remained still. You let me continue.

The coldness of your tongue.

It tasted like the flame of a match. I closed my eyes; abruptly I was shoved back. Immediately a hard blow landed on my lips. It felt like a star had exploded in my mouth. I gripped the floor, prostrate on it, my mouth agape. It was incredible, the pain shooting through me, all I could do in its intensity was hang my mouth open. Instantly my tongue swelled up, and I felt something granular, like sand, slide down its length. Dark, oddly black drops of blood dripped down onto the tatami mats. Pain. Wretched, grievous pain, and with it — a sense of clarity. The lucidity of it was almost welcome. You lay into me, you kicked and you stamped. In the stomach, in the back, on my thighs, my knees, calves, back, head... You collided into me without uttering a single word. Laughter erupted out of me. It was wretchedly painful, but clear. I received what you had to give me. I received this clarity. Better this than the uncertainty of waiting; ten times, a hundred times better. At the sound of my laughter, you stepped back and stood still, silent. I laughed and laughed until I was completely depleted, then I turned round on my side. Let's sleep now. Sleep now.

Once I'd closed my eyes I couldn't open them again. With every beat of my heart the pain rippled out, in thudding, booming waves: the explosion in my mouth sending tremors throughout my body. My chin wet, I concentrated on every surge of torturous sensation. Then I became aware of other sounds. The sound of you picking up your bag from the floor, putting on your shoes, opening the door, and going down the wooden stairs overlaid with steel plates, not bothering to close the door behind you. I merely lay there, listening. Someone was pounding on the wall from the next room. I couldn't tell how long they had been at it, but they went on pounding and pounding, again and again and again and again.

—

I have not laid eyes on you since.

After returning to Korea, the first thing I did as soon as I'd made my way out of the airport was to go in search of you at your address. The address at which my postcards would have arrived. The house was on a hill, a long trek up from the bus stop. I pressed the bell of the shabby entrance, and a woman answered. I asked for you by name through the interphone, at first the woman didn't seem to understand who I was looking for, then she asked if I was looking for the young man who'd been renting a room from her a while back. She said you had packed up and left the room about a year ago. A year was too long a time. It meant you had sought me out in Japan after you'd quit this place. This was where I lost you, then. I had lost you.

Where are you now?

Are you back?

Or are you somewhere across the sea, still.

Did you come across the same things I saw there? The silent drummer, the girl in her red jacket crying

shi'ne, shi'ne: did you see them too? And in your seeing them did they also see you. From where do I start
enquiring after you? To whom do I ask after you.

Now and then I dream that you are dying.

Waking up I am relieved to find it was a dream,
but you will die sooner or later.

When I think you may already be dead, I am terrified.

And yet, in the end, your death may be what I'm
waiting for.

This is what I have got to thinking lately.

I hope this postcard reaches you one day.

Until news of your death comes and finds me, I
will go on writing to you, and waiting.

Believing that you are somewhere out there still.

Believing you to be alive.

Until I receive news of your death, you are alive. I
wait, believing this to be true.

You're out there somewhere.

It's been too long since I saw you.

—

Sora and Nana have been mulling over Geumju ssi's
jesa recently.

Anyone who lays store by custom as a crucial element of jesa might find Sora and Nana's approach to

the ritual absurd. Ever since I've known them, the sisters have held their jesa by placing, on the anniversary of their father's death, food and drinks under the window closest to the north, in secret. A glass of clear alcohol, a bowl of rice; sometimes a bowl of soup is added alongside this, other times it's the plainly weird stuff that makes it up there, from flower-shaped red-bean cakes to popsicles and banana pudding. While they lived with Aeja Ajumoni, they had prepared the table at night when their mother slept. Back then they could only leave the table out for a short while before promptly putting it away. There was barely time to write out the jibang for the wall. I ask them what the plan is for this year's jesa. They look at each other, then Sora answers, we're not sure.

They want us to take back the jesa from them.

They?

Well, Grandmother.

Apparently, their grandmother had got in touch as the death anniversary of Geumju ssi neared. Until now his jesa had been held together with the rest of the family's, she had said, but now she wished her grandchildren to take back their father's jesa.

Now they want us to take over, they're always calling the shots, aren't they, Nana complains, then she asks how exactly one goes about reclaiming jesa.

Maybe we give them some silk in exchange, Sora says.

Why silk.

Because of the story; you know, the one about giving silk and receiving jesa.

That's right, an older sister who received some silk from the younger sister in exchange for...

For her dreams.

Was that how it went.

Probably.

Was it though.

———

On the anniversary of Geumju ssi's death, I closed up shop early and headed over to theirs.

Nana opened the door with flour-covered hands. The two of them had each taken a day's leave to prepare the jesa, and judging from the abundant smell of food that filled the house they had been at it for most of the day. Aeja Ajumoni being absent this year, the table was much bigger than usual, and the number of dishes, too, had increased substantially. There was rice and a meat broth and rice cake, and they'd also pan-fried meatballs and tossed namul and steamed yellow croaker, Nana boasted. And she'd even made sanjeok for the first time ever, she said, and lifted the lid of a pot to show me the meat and vegetable skewers; it looked like she'd used a generous amount of soy sauce, it looked quite salty.

Rice to the west, broth to the east.

Dates and heads to the east, chestnuts and tails to the west.

While Sora and I arranged the dishes this way and that and set the jesa table properly, Nana sat down in a comfortable position and wrote out the jibang with a brush pen. Sora looked on for a bit, and remarked that Nana had written the characters out just like that back in the day, too. Hyeongo Haksaeng Bugoon Shinwi.

I can write it in Hanja now, I'm just choosing not to, Nana said rather primly with the brush in hand. I don't want to alarm Geumju ssi by writing in Hanja after all this time, so I'm sticking to the way we used to do it. After the table was set and the jibang was put up, we lit the candles and used their flames to light the incense; then the two sisters offered up liquor and bows.

Father, Sora spoke up.

It must have been confusing for you each year, having two jesa tables offered up. Having to wonder where to visit first.

From now on you need only come here, Nana said.

You can come straight here, Sora said.

After that we left the table out all night, and settled next to it, to while away the evening chilling out and eating leftovers. We left the incense to burn out, only lighting new candles now and then to illuminate the room. Nana lay down on her side, saying her stomach was weighing on her, and talked about a news item that I seemed to recall having heard one day. It was about these three comets that were hurtling towards Earth. The comets were approaching Earth, according to the news, and four months from now two of the three would narrowly skirt the earth's atmosphere. Isn't that old news, though, I asked, but Nana opened her eyes wide and said it had been announced just yesterday. But I'm quite sure this was on the news a while back, I said, and Sora chimed in to say that was probable, too. Since comets are always coming at us. So something similar could have happened a while back as well, she said.

You know what, Nana went on.

Before, when I heard news like this I thought that was it for Earth, Earth was doomed, and didn't think much about it or feel much of anything. But these days I can't think about it in the same way. It would be too unfair for the baby to be born, only for the world to end like that. After all the effort of birth, after all the time it's taken for the baby to come out into the world, if the world was to just end.

Why would it end, Sora asks.

Why would you think the world's going to end.

Cause I'm worried.

Why would you worry about something like that.

Well, that's the sort of thing that worries me these days.

I said, you know how dinosaurs disappeared.

Yeah.

How they became extinct.

Yep, extinct.

You'd think it was instantaneous, extinction, but in fact they say it took millions of years.

Really?

They disappeared gradually, over tens of millions of years.

That's rather a long time.

It is.

Things don't go to pot that quickly.

I mean the world doesn't, I added.

You don't think it'll be torture to take that long to disappear?, Nana asked.

You prefer if it happens in an instant?

No.

So let's go to ruin over the long term, then.

Must we go to ruin?

I'm just saying it doesn't happen that quickly.

Tired from all the cooking they'd done that day, Sora and Nana soon nodded off. I looked at the ceiling as it gently undulated in the dusky light. From either end of the jesa table, the two candles smeared the surrounding walls with irregular stains of incandescence. The melted wax spluttered as it burned. Sora and Nana were breathing quietly. It was silent. A desolate silence, as if the moment the candles died out the room itself would be snuffed out. It felt familiar, like something I'd witnessed since childhood.

I thought of the room, the room where you had come to stay.

Would it be there still.

It had existed there for decades, well before I'd got to know it, so yes, it was likely still there.

Or so I believe.

Will I ever revisit it.

Will I ever meet you again.

If I were to meet you again one day, would you find me loveable, would you look on me with love.

So that one day I will come to say yes, my being born was a good thing — will that day ever come.

It's been a long while since I saw you.

NANA

娜 娜

I had a dream.

I awoke from sleep to find a great moon looming outside the window.

It's a big window, but the moon's gigantic and won't fit in the square. I sit up under my blanket and gaze at the moon. I am enveloped in its white moonbeams. I open my mouth, I say the words: it's the moon; immediately the moon starts to flicker. Ripples skim across its surface in waves of concentric circles, as if the moon were a reflection on water. One minute it assumes a jolly, tickled air, then one of peevishness, then it's being as coy and charming as you like, and here it is now, settling back to its limpid, placid self. How unusual, I murmur, and right then I sense something inside pushing long at me, and I wake up, only for real this time.

The room is dark, and warm.

I'm tangled up in a blanket someone's fetched for me. I must have fallen asleep without realising it. The baby gives another long kick right beneath my belly button. It's got into the habit of moving around at night now. During the day when I'm up and about, the baby lies in wait quietly, and when night falls and Nana's the one lying in wait, that's when the baby starts to move about. Sometimes it gets to be too much, the movements waking Nana up as they have tonight. On these nights it happens not once but three or four times throughout, disrupting sleep and draining me of all energy. So Nana's used to placing her hands round her belly button before going to bed, and saying, Mummy's sleepy, Mummy's going to sleep now so no big movements, please. Nana's gotten to calling herself Mummy now. And is quite comfortable with it, too. It's all very unusual. Even Sora, who's been visibly uneasy with Nana addressing herself as Mummy, has lately got to placing a hand on Nana's belly and saying, you see how inflexible your Mum is, so it's on you to be gentle with her. That in itself is really quite unusual, too.

I think back to the moon in the dream.

The latest in I'm not sure how many taemong I've had. Recalling the bashful flutterings of the moon now, I feel something catch in my chest. So that's what it is, Nana thinks to herself. This is what it means to be choked up. Feeling the knotting of your heart, the sudden binds occurring severally and all at once. A trussed heart.

But it was definitely a great big moon.

If a moon ever does get that near, there's no question Earth will be doomed.

The moon itself would be beyond beautiful, but regardless, Nana and the world would undoubtedly perish.

Nana used to imagine this is what she'd see on the very last day. If you could be witness to such a sight, the end of the world wouldn't entirely be gloom and doom, she'd thought then.

But she can no longer think as calmly and complacently about the same things. Now she feels the world may end at any moment, and that that end will be so agonising and gruesome for everyone, she can't help but be anxious about the precariousness of it all. Maybe she's more attuned to the dearness of things now. And in expanding her list of things to cherish, Nana may have wound up a frailer person than before.

In ten million years there could well be a hundred thousand Nanas.

A time span in which Nana will recur a hundred

thousand times.

A hundred thousand recurring Nanas, there's a nauseating thought. But within those hundred thousand reiterations there's bound to be laughing Nana. Nana laughing. And crying raging longing quaking in fear shrinking with shyness pouting moping, and again: laughing crying rejoicing biding her time and so on.

Ten million years.

People aren't dinosaurs and may reach their end in a shorter time span than the dinosaurs ever did.

Whether the flipside is also possible, whether people might meet their end more slowly than dinosaurs, I haven't the faintest idea. But in either case the world's end will befall us only gradually, and this will give Nana time to think properly about things. There's time yet.

—

Aeja continues to phone them, late at night.

Poor thing.

There's no use trying.

None of it matters.

It's all futile.

Trifles and things of no consequence.

That's life for you: it can be halted at any moment,

and trifles are all any human life ever amounts to, she says, and Nana does find herself, for the most part, agreeing with her. People *are* trifling, their lives meagre and fleeting. But this, Nana thinks, is also what makes them loveable.

For keeping on amid the inconsequential.

For abiding, at times gladly and at times in sadness.

And she also considers this.

She wonders if insignificance is in fact, or necessarily, bad.

Sora, Nana, Naghi Oraboni, Sunja Ajumoni, the baby, Aeja: all may well be insignificant so far as the world's concerned, mere fleeting and therefore inconsequential beings.

But the more she thinks about it, the more it seems untrue that by the same token they're therefore not worth cherishing.

The baby's settled in for the night now. Sora and Oraboni are breathing easily in their sleep. Everyone is slumbering. I sit in the dark, lending my ear to these tenuous sounds. Day will break before long.

I'll go on.

This edition published in the United Kingdom by Tilted Axis Press in 2018. This translation was funded by Arts Council England.

tiltedaxispress.com

First published 2014 in Korean by Changbi as 계속해보겠습니다 (Gyesokkehbogetsumnida).

ISBN (paperback)   9781911284208
ISBN (ebook)   9781911284192

A catalogue record for this book is available from the British Library.

Edited by Saba Ahmed
Cover design by Soraya Gilanni Viljoen
Typesetting and ebook production by Simon Collinson
Printed and bound by Clays Ltd, Elcograf S.p.A.

The publication and translation of this book is supported by the Daesan Foundation.

Supported using public funding by
**ARTS COUNCIL
ENGLAND**

ABOUT TILTED AXIS PRESS

Founded in 2015 and based in Sheffield and London, Tilted Axis is a not-for-profit press on a mission to shake up contemporary international literature.

Tilted Axis publishes the books that might not otherwise make it into English, for the very reasons that make them exciting to us — artistic originality, radical vision, the sense that here is something new.

Tilting the axis of world literature from the centre to the margins allows us to challenge that very division. These margins are spaces of compelling innovation, where multiple traditions spark new forms and translation plays a crucial role.

As part of carving out a new direction in the publishing industry, Tilted Axis is also dedicated to improving access. We're proud to pay our translators the proper rate, and to operate without unpaid interns.

We hope you find this fantastic book as thrilling and beguiling as we do, and if you do, we'd love to know.

tiltedaxispress.com

@TiltedAxisPress